THE SPY GAME

THE SPY GAME

A NOVEL

GEORGINA HARDING

BLOOMSBURY

NEW YORK · BERLIN · LONDON

Published by Bloomsbury USA, New York

All papers used by Bloomsbury USA are natural, recyclable products made from wood grown in well-managed forests. The manufacturing processes conform to the environmental regulations of the country of origin.

LIBRARY OF CONGRESS CATALOGING-IN-PUBLICATION DATA

Harding, Georgina, 1955-
The spy game : a novel / Georgina Harding. – 1st U.S. ed.
p. cm.
ISBN-13: 978-1-59691-589-3 (hardcover)
ISBN-10: 1-59691-589-7 (hardcover)
1. Cold War–Psychological aspects–Fiction. 2. Adolescence–Fiction. 3.
Psychological fiction. I. Title.

PR6108.A724S79 2009
823'.92–dc22
2008032697

First U.S. Edition 2009

1 3 5 7 9 10 8 6 4 2

Typeset by Hewer Text UK Ltd, Edinburgh
Printed in the United States of America by Quebecor World Fairfield

For Nellie,
and for Kay

1

Fog that morning, a freezing fog; the flagstones dark and slippery outside the door. I shall always associate my mother with fog. Once she went up to London in one of the last pea-soupers, I cannot have been more than six then, and came back on the train late. She drove home and came in beneath the bright overhead light in the hall and talked about it, and when she took off her silk headscarf I thought that I saw a remnant of the fog shaken off it, a dull spray that fell away off the gleam of the silk. I saw it like a horror.

It was there, I told her. The smog. She had brought it home.

My mother looked in the hall mirror as if to check, smiled a dazzling smile into the glass and shaped up her hair where it had been flattened by the scarf.

'All gone now.'

The smog in London had a greenish-yellowish colour because of the poison it contained, that made you cough if you did not wear a mask and made fragile people die. The smog was famous so you remembered when people talked about it.

The fog at home was plain grey country fog, dead leaves and cow smell in it and the hollow sound of milking in the farm across the road. No poison there but numbness, a numbness that you knew from other, forgotten days, that seeped into grass and wood and stone and skin, and made them all the same, until feeling was gone along with the sight of the village and the valley and the hills, as if these no longer existed and there was only this one numb place and no other to be known.

And yet the hills were there, even if I could not see them. I knew that they were there; and close, not remote at all. The road rose steeply out where the houses ended, up round bends and through close woods to the ridge and the high open land beyond it. Up there on the fog-covered hills there would be ice, on the surfaces of the roads that had been wet yesterday with all the week's rain, hidden ribbons of ice on the slopes, on the bends where water had run down in black streams on the asphalt. There was a skin of ice on the dips in the stone path. Later I would go out in my boots and smash it like glass but now I stood huddled on the step still warm from bed and felt the cold on my bare face and through the soles of my slippers, penetrating and pushing away the sleep.

'Don't stand out there, Anna, you will catch your death.' The ineradicable pattern of German in my mother's voice. 'Run on in and get dressed.'

Cold, waking me up. A Monday in January during the Cold War. A sting in the air that touched closer than the kiss she gave me, which was no more than a brush of breath and powdered cheek, and a pursing of new red lips just so far from the skin as to leave no mark, and I stood in my slippers on the doorstep and had already as a memory or a dream the waxy scented smell of her as she started up the car and ran it awhile with the exhaust puffing while she scraped windscreen and windows, and then got in and closed the door and seemed to wave, though the scraped patch was small and it was hard to see, and drove away. Her lights were gone, into the cold.

What I did next was done with the deliberateness of a child suddenly responsible for herself. I went back in as I had been told, pushing the big bolt across the bottom of the front door that I must not open to strangers. I finished a bowl of Rice Krispies that had grown soggy and then went upstairs and again I did as I had been told. I put on a warm vest and long socks and jeans. There was a green mohair jumper that I kept after that for years, until it was too small and worn through in places and dangled broken threads that caught in things, but I would not let it go. I put it on that morning because of the cold. Later I would wear it in almost any weather. I folded my pyjamas and put them under the pillow, tidied the bed and pulled up the bed-spread, arranged my animals upon it. From downstairs came the clumsy sound of Margaret doing the cleaning, moving things round as she dusted the sitting room. (Useless girl, my mother would say, stroking the top of some table and inspecting the dust that collected on her fingertips. Has she no eyes with which to see?) I slipped by, slipped down past the open door to the room, where Margaret had her back turned and was unwinding the cord of the Hoover. I found my satchel in the kitchen, took my coat from its hook in the hall and let myself out at the back, pulling out the mittens and hat that were stuffed in the pockets and shoving them on soon as the cold hit. I walked to Susan's, walked fast in spite of the fog, head down, scarcely needing to see the way as I walked it so often, around the side of the house, down the stone path and along the road, and then through the gate into her front garden, and the fog was thick and the ice was thin, scrunching into mud underfoot, and Mrs Lacey let me in as she always did and a little later we drove to school. Mrs Lacey drove slowly, rubbing the windscreen and leaning forward over the steering wheel as if those few inches made all the difference to what she could see. And all day the fog held. It was there like a milky breath beyond the classroom windows, at break, at lunch, when Mrs Lacey took us back at the end of the day, the headlamps lighting it before the car. Even when it got dark and the fire was lit and the curtains were drawn, I knew that the fog was there.

The Times, Monday 9 January 1961. Price sixpence. (Going back now, going over these things, I read the newspapers for that day.) The front page is given over to the Classi-

6

fieds. How faceless it was then, the front page of *The Times*, a full broadsheet page of solid type, small-type lists cramped across seven tight columns: Births, Marriages, Deaths, Personal (and yet how impersonal), Motor Cars Etc., Shipping, Agriculture.

PALMER on 7 January 1961, peacefully, after an accident, HILDA BEATRICE, widow of Lieut. Col. C. H. PALMER . . .

Notice of a ship of the Blue Star Line disembarking London via Lisbon for Brazil, Uruguay and Argentina, exclusively first-class.

The news does not begin to appear until page six. *Two Climbers Found Dead. Union Plan for Car Industry. Child Drowns in Roadwork Trench.* The Portland story is slipped in amongst the rest. *Victory Assured for President de Gaulle. Five People on Secrets Act Charge. General McKeown in Leopoldville.* It runs to a few standard phrases, no more. The reporting is quaintly dated: the plain headlines, the conventional formulations, the formality with which people are named, the images which are pinched and small, head-and-shoulders photographs mainly of the Prime Minister and dignitaries and people with titles. All of it is respectful, restrained, clipped like the BBC voices of the time, drilled in objectivity. *Suspects charged under the Official Secrets Act, held at Bow Street Police Station . . .*

The same news must have been on the radio that morning. It is possible that my mother heard it in the kitchen before she left, but she was early and in a rush, so it is more likely that she would have heard it in the car as she drove. There is nowhere lonelier than a car in a thick fog. She would have had the radio on for company, driving so slowly that every turn in the known road seemed alien to her, delayed, out of place, the lights of oncoming cars looming weirdly towards her, the road surface revealing itself too late, having of necessity to be trusted. She would have heard the voices in the background as she concentrated on where she was going, looking for some movement in the air, hoping that the fog would lift on the hilltops or across the next valley or when the hills were passed.

The Times' forecast has the fog in the west of England dense but clearing slowly; the roads icy at first; the wind light, variable. I remember no wind, and the fog did not clear. In Gloucestershire where I spent that day the air remained entirely still, as if it was a day that didn't happen.

If someone had told me that it was a day that I must remember always, I would of course have made it different. I was old enough to know the conventions of these things. If for example my mother had been a soldier and there had been a proper war, then I would have stood at the door and marked it all. (And if she had not been who she was, and if she was on the right side.) I would have marked the shine in her eyes, the braveness of her smile, the set of her shoulders in the big tweed coat. I would have stood that extra moment gazing into the fog after the car's red lights had melted into it; made a picture for my memory of a tall pale girl in a dressing gown, pink slippers and a warm bed behind her but no one else in the house.

And after, I would have not have gone to school but stayed at home. Just myself, alone. No Margaret there to flatten the atmosphere. There was something so mundane about Margaret – mundane was a new word, one that I had heard Mrs Lacey say in her high, ringing voice, and I had held it though I was not quite sure of its meaning and applied it to Margaret, Margaret with her heaviness and her thick legs and her acne. To be eight years old, just a few days over eight and alone in the house would have been much finer.

I would have done something solitary. I would have taken out some cards and sat down on the carpet in the sitting room and played patience. Mrs Lacey had taught us to play a game of patience that she called Chinaman. She said that in Singapore there was a Chinaman who sat on the street and invited you to play the game, and you paid him money and he gave you the pack of cards, and if you got more than thirteen cards out he gave you the money back and you kept the cards as well, and you had won. That didn't sound so many, thirteen, but it was hard to get. Mrs Lacey said that it was to do with odds. The Chinaman was good at sums and could work out the odds. He wouldn't sit out on the street and play the game if he did not know that he would mostly win. And yet every now and then the odds fell in the player's favour, and that made you feel good. So I would lay out the cards, seven along with the first upturned, six the next line, and so on, and play the game through, and when I had worked down the pack once – just once, the Chinaman was strict about that and to go on would be cheating – I would gather the cards up and shuffle and deal once more.

Again and again, until the game came out, I would lay the lines of cards against the pattern of the Persian rug before the fire, and the fire would be burning (some invisible hand must have been there to light it for me) and there would be the glow of the fire and the circle of light from the lamp, or perhaps, as the day passed, clearing slowly, a low beam of winter sun breaking through the grey beyond the window.

I'd deal the cards and they'd go down crisp. I'd gather them up and deal again. All the time I would have known that at any moment the policeman might come, or the postman, some man in uniform with the news in him, holding the words back like he held his bicycle, like you'd hold back a young dog from a stranger; and the fair-haired girl who stood at the door (a heroine to myself, having a quality of calm and self-possession beyond given age) would have known at once what words they were by the look in his face.

If she had been a soldier, it would have been black-and-white; black-and-white like the postman's telegram, because this after all was 1961, because I was eight, because war was the confrontation of good and evil and the soldiers on our side were heroes, because I watched television, because we did not have colour then. Clear-cut, not the muddle it became: the hanging around at the Laceys' house long after school, the staying for tea – though that in itself was nothing strange, I was often there for tea – the being there even after Mr Lacey came home and poured his gin and tonic and turned on the News while the phone rang, then having a bed made up in Susan's room and staying the night. Your parents won't be back till late, they want you to stay here with us. And all that evening beneath the surface, the knowledge of something big unspoken, of the falseness of smiles and the coding of words.

Two days earlier, the previous Saturday, 7 January 1961, twenty minutes past three in the afternoon. Two people come through a ticket barrier at Waterloo Station. The man who is watching notes them soon as they get out of the train, though there is nothing particular about this pair to set them apart from other men and women on platform fourteen. Perhaps he, like the eight others on the train itself and in the street who have been set to watch them on this and past days, recognises them from photographs. Perhaps he has observed the same couple before. Of course he has been trained how to look: to identify what distinguishes an individual's appearance, to register hair colour, eyes, build, pattern of movement, to estimate height and weight and put together a precise and communicable description. To anyone else what is most apparent about this couple is their ordinariness, the ordinariness of so many of the passengers beneath the platform lamps and the late daylight that seeps through the dirty glass roof of the station, drab men and women with winter overcoats and brown hats and tired London faces.

There are other papers besides *The Times*. I have ordered the *Guardian*, the *Telegraph* and the *Daily Mail* for the same dates. *The Times* is available digitally; the others only on microfiche. The film comes on old-fashioned spools, a bore to load and to crank through, and then to position and focus. Here and there one of the papers has a picture, small by today's standards, poorly rendered on paper and worse on the screen: a man or woman, just a face, the subjects grouped in some old snapshot, an item of evidence, the scene of the arrest. Enlarge the image and it disintegrates into no more than a series of formations, concentrations, of grey dots. The library where I work is stuffy, windowless. A dozen strangers breathe the same air in dim booths, yawn above the soporific tap of keyboards.

The watchers, the watched, the passers-by.

One form merging into the next, heads passing, shoulder brushing against shoulder, gloved hands holding bags, hands in pockets, dark shoes treading an intricate and abstract intersecting pattern across the station floor. Nothing to indicate who is who; no sign of the veiled concentration in the eyes of MI5 agents, the alertness that must surely run like an adrenaline current behind the bland faces of the spies, the anxieties, hopes, intentions of any of the travellers around.

Where the crowd funnels at the exit on to the Waterloo Road, the watchers hasten suddenly, looking about them, keeping track in the confusion, to relax only as the couple separate from the rest and become a distinct pair walking south. And the watchers slow again, hands back in pockets, sauntering now some way behind, unseen by their subjects, never seen but only watching as the police cars swerve in.

'The hunt is over. Scotland Yard for you!' says Superintendent 'Moonraker' Smith, spycatcher extraordinary.

Did a policeman ever really speak like that?

The newspapers bring back that time not only by their meaning but by their style: the clichés of the popular press, the restraint of the broadsheets. In this I hear the talk of my father and those around him, the generation who grew up in the war and composed themselves so carefully afterwards and put it behind them; who established about them what they saw as the civilised rhythm of post-war life, which was perhaps a shadow of life before: a drink at six, dressing for dinner (being who they were, being the class that they were, reassuring themselves of its changelessness even then on the cusp of change), the Nine O'Clock News, Sunday lunch. The newspaper advertisements represent the time as effectively as the stories. There are advertisements for Manikin Cigars, Mappin & Webb, Land Rover, 'Good old Johnnie Walker', illustrated with line drawings and photographs that appear now to have a parochial naivety; advertisements for British things conjuring a peculiarly British reality: familiar, named, secure, where everything and everyone, child and adult, had their place, and what did not fit was not acknowledged to exist.

The booth next to mine was empty when I came. I chose this position because of that, and because it was at the end of the line. It has been so long since I have done research like this, not since I was a student. Easier not to be observed fumbling with the spools; nice anyway to have space about me. Now a young Indian woman in jeans and a turquoise tunic has taken the spot, placed file and notebook on the desk and is taking out the first of a small stack of films. She looks as awkward at it as I was earlier, reading the instructions taped to the side of the booth, threading, unthreading, setting the whole clanking thing into motion and winding the first film back so far that it winds right off the spool.

'Do you know how to work these things?' An apologetic whisper.

'Only just.'

Her voice is that of an educated Indian from India; she looks earnest, with heavy brows and dark-rimmed spectacles, bangles on her arm. A Ph.D. student perhaps, not so young as all that – as one gets older, other women begin to seem younger than they are – or a lecturer even, someone with a proper reason to be here.

There is nothing for it but to get up and try to help, ineffectually, until a librarian comes and saves us. Then I can return and begin a systematic working through of all the sources: the referenced dates of arrest, trial and sentencing; details of identities, contacts, methods. Just in case there is something there.

I had expected there to be a canteen, somewhere to eat, at least a pleasant café near by. Whenever I come to London these days I notice how many nice cafés there are, people eating out everywhere, sitting out even in April eating Mediterranean food; so much more happening than in the few years I lived here in the Seventies. But this place where the library is can hardly be called London; it is only some shabby northern suburb, whose name one knows from the tube map, out almost to Edgware on the Northern Line. The institutional red brick of the building seems misplaced on the poor terraced street, no shops in sight but a dingy newsagent and a greasy café of a kind I have not visited in thirty years, not since the days when I was a student myself. I order what I might have ordered then: strong tea and a bacon sandwich, on bread, not toast, white factory bread with the grease soaking into it. At least today I am hungry enough for that.

The café is busy. It must really be the only one around. The Indian woman is sitting alone and I take a seat at the same table.

She has nothing but a cup of tea.

'I did not know,' she says, 'what I should be eating here.'

She does not know what an outsider I am here, how rarely I come to London, that I scarcely ever meet people like herself. Will she be Muslim, Hindu, vegetarian? No bacon, anyway. I recommend egg and chips.

'I have a research grant,' the Indian woman says, looking out of the window, where a bus passes in the rain. 'Six weeks in London. I have never been to London before.'

'Ah. Well, you must see some other places besides this.'

'I shall, if my work allows.'

'Definitely you must take some time to look around.'

'And how long will you be working here?'

'I don't know,' I say, though I do in fact. I have three days here in London and then I shall fly to Berlin. 'I'm here in London for a bit, and then I'm going to Germany and Poland, well, not quite Poland actually but Russia.'

'It sounds very interesting.'

'Oh, it isn't really. It isn't my job or anything. I'm wasting my time really. It's just that now I have time to waste. My daughter's grown up, she's off my hands now, and my husband said I might as well do it. It's nothing important, you see, just a family matter. Just something I thought I might find out about, now that I have the time.'

It was to come out in court that the couple under surveillance had reached Waterloo by an unnecessarily devious route. There was no suggestion as to whether this was the result of whim or accident, or whether it was a deliberate but amateurish attempt to shake off anyone who might be tailing them.

They had come on the train from Salisbury, though they might have chosen to take one direct from Weymouth, having driven first as far as Salisbury and then left their car there – because of the icy roads, they were to say, but then the train itself had to be re-routed around Basingstoke, where previous heavy rain had washed away the line. If they had intended to do much shopping up in London, they no longer had the time. They must limit the trip to a threepenny bus ride to the market in East Street, Walworth, and be back by four-thirty for the meeting they had arranged.

Their names were Harry Houghton and Ethel Elizabeth Gee, though Ethel was generally known as Bunty, the newspapers recorded. Both were employees at the Portland Admiralty Underwater Weapons Establishment, Bunty a clerical assistant of the lowest grade in the drawing-office records section, Harry a clerical officer in the innocuous-sounding Port Auxiliary Repair Unit, where he had access to Admiralty fleet orders and charts and particulars of ships. The two of them occasionally made these trips up to London, and once or twice they had stayed a night. (One of the newspapers refers to Bunty as a 'friendly spinster', which seems a coy way of saying that she slept with Harry and that at the hotel they visited she slipped a ring on her finger and pretended to be his wife.)

On this occasion it appeared that they were not planning to stay. Perhaps Bunty had to be home for the three old people she cared for: her eighty-year-old mother, her bedridden Aunt Bessie, her Uncle John (or Jack as some of the newspapers had it). Possibly Harry had some other intention. Surveillance on a previous trip he had made to meet his contact in London alone had picked up a comment about a girl from South Africa. The implication that he had been two-timing Bunty was the sort of thing people would have expected of spies, even if he was fifty-five and balding and had been living until recently in a caravan.

On returning to Waterloo Road Harry and Bunty crossed to the corner by the Old Vic. There a man walked swiftly to them and they shook hands. Gordon Lonsdale, as he called himself (real name K. T. Molody) was dark and stocky, with a style and spark to him that the others lacked. His manners too had charm, for he turned to Bunty and offered instantly to take the shopping basket that she was carrying. A normal thing, she said she thought it was, for a gentleman to do.

I know the place. I have been to the Old Vic a few times, when I lived in London and once or twice since. I know the street. It is a bleak street even now, the pavement running between the long blank wall of the theatre and the grimy breadth of Waterloo Road, the sound of traffic and the fumes holding there between the road and the high wall. It would have been even bleaker then, with the street line on the other side broken still by bomb and building sites. The only bright things to be seen would have been the posters on the theatre walls, advertising the current production. (According to the theatre notices, an unseasonal *A*

Midsummer Night's Dream, the saturday matinée playing within the plush warmth of the theatre as the spies walked by in the cold.)

It must have been Lonsdale who chose that particular street, since he was the professional. He chose it for its anonymity perhaps, or for the fact that it was wide and straight and open, without corners or doorways or crossings to produce surprises.

He had used it as a rendezvous at least three times before; twice meeting Harry and Bunty together, and once meeting Harry alone. Once he had been observed meeting Harry elsewhere. On all these occasions they had been watched, shadowed, their conversations overheard by discreet couples, idlers, newspaper sellers, some with microphones and tape recorders in coat pockets. For four years now he or his colleagues or masters had summoned Harry by prearranged signals. The signals are of a type that make one laugh, nowadays, so quaint and clichéd they seem. In real life, this happened: a spy summoned by a Hoover brochure coming in the post, or an advertising card (folded in half) for the Scotch House in Knightsbridge, to meetings in the London area, in suburban pubs such as the Maypole in Ditton Road or the Toby Jug in Tolworth, where he must carry a copy of *Punch,* or hold a newspaper in one hand or a glove in the other so that his contact could identify him.

It was almost dark by now, on a January day which had never quite become light, the damp surface of the road beginning to shine before the cars. They walked fast because it was cold, and also perhaps because they were tense and they wanted this over and done with, this meeting which was the greatest moment of danger for them all. Bunty walked between the two men, Lonsdale closest to the wall on the pavement side carrying her basket. Did they speak? Of what? Of the next meeting, of the delays of the journey, the rotten weather that made travelling such a nuisance, raising their voices as two lorries passed, a bus, making it hard to hear?

And then cars pulled up and men were coming at them shouting.

'The next thing I knew we were absolutely swooped on,' Bunty says from the witness box. 'At that time, I could not imagine what it was. I thought they were Teddy boys. Mr [Superintendent] Smith stood out. I could not imagine how one gentleman came to be mixed up with a lot of Teddy boys. There was so much noise I could not hear a word. I did not know who they were.'

At the time all she said was, 'Oh.'

Harry said, 'What?'

Lonsdale said not a word.

In her shopping basket were found four Admiralty test pamphlets, each of many foolscap pages; undeveloped film containing photographs of two hundred and thirty pages of *Particulars of War Vessels*, including specifications of *HMS Dreadnought*, Britain's first nuclear submarine; a package from the newsagent's and a tin of tongue.

'Peter, sweetheart, how can you waste such a day as this? Out with you now, and take some air!'

That was what our mother would have said. She used to say it so often I could remember precisely the rhythm in her voice, the bright tone that carried clear from room to room across the house.

Peter was home from boarding school and it was summer. It must have been that first summer after we were alone but from the sort of day it was it could have been any one of them. All those summers when I look back on them seem the same.

Peter didn't go outside and there was no one to make him. Our mother used to worry over Peter because he was so pale and thin. Our father, on the days when he was home, did not seem to notice. He was gentle with us but sometimes that seemed a passing-by, as if we did not quite touch, and the soil and the leaves and the stems of the flowers in the garden were more tangible to him than we ourselves. All the light hours of the day he seemed to be in the garden, and when the days were long, supper was late so that we had filled ourselves on bread and peanut butter before he remembered that he must come in and cook.

On the days that he went to work, I used to get up at the same time and see him off, Peter a little later. Then Margaret came, each morning, and often Susan came to play or sometimes we went to Susan's house; and when Margaret was gone Mrs Lacey fed us lunch and after that the two of us went pretty much where we pleased, though Mrs Lacey was there if we needed her, if we were hungry or cut ourselves. The routine had come about so naturally that it never occurred to us to think that the adults must have talked and planned (discussed and decided as they had so many other things) and arranged the structure of our lives. For ourselves, we knew no control but only eased into a freedom of a kind that the adult world did not recognise, that was the unspoken freedom of the mother-less. No one to be answerable to, every minute of the day, no one to make us put our boots on before we went out, no one watching. When my mother was there I can remember saying, ten times a day, 'What shall I do now?' and waiting in all the vacancy of a child's boredom for a bright reply. That was not so any more. We were ourselves alone and thought for ourselves, and there were no words to it. We just did what we did.

Peter made aeroplanes. Each Saturday morning Dad took us into Cheltenham and Peter bought a new model kit and a wartime comic book, and in the week that followed he made the plane. He had British ones and German ones, and a few American bombers, and hung them from the ceiling of his room. He knew all about them, when they were built and where they fought and what kind of guns they had. When he was younger the whole house sounded with the dogfights he staged from his bed, with rattles of guns and ack-ack and dives and cries of *Achtung!*

On this day the house is quiet. Only the two of us in it and Peter intent in the playroom making the latest plane. I was singing a moment ago, out in the sun. I love to sing. I was singing songs round and round so that they never ended, singing out in the garden and in through the French windows, and now that I have stopped the empty rooms have fallen back more silent than before.

'What's the matter, Peter?'

Peter sits hunched with his hair falling to his eyes. The plane lies still in pieces on the table, only parts of it made. His face is blotchy, his hands tight and awkward with anger.

'Has your plane gone wrong?'

Till then I think we had not spoken of her. Not seriously at least, not in any way that I can remember. Peter had come home immediately afterwards, and we saw each other then, and we spent the various school holidays together, but we had not talked about it.

'How do we know she's dead?'

His eyes were shiny so that I did not look into them. He was almost crying. I looked at his fingers instead, how they were white with the pressure. They held the wing of the plane so tight that I was afraid he might break it and then he would cry for sure.

'Because they told us.'

Actually, but I could not have said this to him, I knew before they told me. I had had the thought from the moment of the phone call, when I was sitting playing cards with Susan and the News was on the television, and Mrs Lacey in the hallway outside the sitting room door said, 'When?' and Mrs Lacey's voice had a crack in it, which failed to resonate like a cracked bowl, and though she had tried to make the flat word sound ordinary its significance had seeped like a gas into the air of the adjoining room. And Mr Lacey was swearing for some reason, and not paying attention to her. He was looking at the television screen, angry at something he saw there.

'Because they told us,' Peter repeated, but the certainty had gone from the words.

Peter was collected now, more his usual self. He put the wing down. He began to peel the dried glue off his fingertips, stripping it off like skin and laying it on the spread newspaper on the table.

'That's just what they said. It doesn't have to be so just because they said it.'

He had his authority back now, the elder brother making statements to his sister. Usually when Peter said things he was right. He lived in a boy's sure world of knowledge and facts, names and dates and numbers. He could identify a make of car or an aeroplane, could quote the height of Everest or Freddie Trueman's bowling figures. He must explain. I did not speak but waited for him to explain.

'Think, Anna. What did they actually say?'

'What did they say to you?'

'Oh, nothing much. Just that Dad was coming to take me out. And I thought that was odd because it was a Tuesday. Then Dad came and Matron packed some things and we got in the car.'

Not what was said but what was done, that was what Peter told. In that case I would not tell either.

Daphne Lacey had to break the news. Even at the time I think I understood that it was hard for her.

Mrs Lacey's manner that morning was strange and sharp. She looked madder than ever. We had always thought secretly that she was a little mad. There was an odd, darting intensity to her, an effect that was heightened by her garish taste in clothes and the smudges of turquoise colour that she put like punctuation marks above her faded eyes. We once saw a bee-eater in the tropical cage at the zoo that had a dash of just that same colour about its eye. Peter whispered that it was like her even though Susan was with us, and Susan couldn't hear us, and we giggled.

The fog had cleared overnight. The morning was bright.

'I think I'll take Benjy for a walk after breakfast. You'll come with me, Anna, won't you, dear?'

We had been told that we must be nice to the Laceys because they came from Malaya and had been in a Jap camp. That meant that they had been prisoners of war. Mrs Lacey had suffered a lot and had lost a child. She looked too old and brittle to be Susan's mother but Margaret said that Susan was a replacement.

Susan was made to stay in, on some pretext or other, and I walked out with Mrs Lacey alone into the bright morning with the poodle beside us. The sun was surprisingly warm. The ice had turned to shiny puddles and there were drips coming off roofs and the dark twigs of trees. We walked down a path that led off the street, and then out past the houses and vegetable patches to a gate and a field. There were sheep in the field and Mrs Lacey put Benjy on a lead and let me hold it. She knew how much I liked to hold the dog. The hill rose smoothly up before the path and rounded off beneath a clear sky.

'There's something I have to tell you, Anna dear. You see, your father telephoned, he called us yesterday, he couldn't come back last night. He asked me to tell you something.'

She didn't put her arm around me or anything, and I did not look at her but only at the trodden path and the grey dog with his wagging dish-brush tail, and the lead connecting me to him.

'Your mummy's gone to heaven.'

I couldn't picture heaven. In the wood the beech trees were bare and if you looked up the sky was a brilliant blue between their branches. Mrs Lacey's heaven would be lush and green and filled with tropical flowers, orange and purple and crimson with petals like tongues.

'There was an accident, he said. He said that it was very quick, very sudden. It must have been over very quickly.'

I do not think that I spoke.

I saw the dog before me and the beeches, and coming out from the trees again beneath the hill I saw the sharpness of the light on the winter grass. These things I would remember. The clean form of the hill and the scar in its side where stone had been quarried and a thorn bush grew in a spiky black outline from a crack in the bared rock. A drystone wall cutting across. I would remember them always.

The church stood where we came back into the village, by the field that was the playground. When we got to it, Mrs Lacey suggested going in.

'Why?'

'I thought it might be nice to say a prayer.'

I had only been into the church once or twice. I liked it from the outside, I liked the sandy warmth of its stone, but inside it was bare and white with long cold windows and an empty smell that must have been made of damp and limewash.

'But we're Catholic. It's not a Catholic church.'

So we walked by the gate and did not stop. Mrs Lacey's face was tight and like a mask with its painted points of colour.

*   *   *

28

'We've only got their word for it,' said Peter. 'We didn't see her, did we? All we know for sure is that she went away, we don't know anything else. We didn't even go to the funeral.'

Peter was a boy and two years older. He had all the toughness in him of his age and of his time away at school. Peter sowed doubts and doubts were power.

'When you think about it, we don't really know anything about her, do we?'

'That's because of her being German, because Daddy met her in Berlin.'

'Yes, but all the same, we should know something. We don't know her family. We don't know anyone who used to know her. We don't even know where she came from, or anything.'

'Yes we do.'

'What?'

'Know where she came from. I know the name of the place. She told me. It was a big place, bigger than Cheltenham. It was called Königsberg.'

'That's what she said, but it's not there. I checked. It isn't on the map. At school, I checked, and it wasn't there.'

'That's not true.'

'Look for yourself if you don't believe me.'

We went to the sitting room and Peter took the atlas down from the big bookcase beside our father's chair. He laid it on the carpet and opened it where Europe began.

'Find it then.'

I looked until my legs ached from being bent on the floor. The afternoon was hot. There was a sort of hum that was a summer day outside but I stayed in and did not notice for a long time that the curtains were still drawn from the night before and that I looked by lamplight. Then I got up and put out the light and drew the heavy curtains back, and saw outside as if it was a foreign country off the map. It was bright, green, behind glass; I could not go there. I went back to my place on the floor. I used to sit on the floor with my legs folded flat, knees together and feet splayed out, but after a long time that began to hurt. I sat some other way. I looked across four wide pages: Central, Eastern Europe, the pale-blue Baltic, the tattered edge of Scandinavia curling above it, the solid blocks of colour beneath. My mother had said that she had lived close to the sea. You could see ships, she had said, from the attic window of her home. I looked at all the names that fanned out from the Baltic coast, in West Germany, East Germany, Poland. I looked at the names inland. Then Peter condescended to show me how the index worked and I put a ruler to the page and worked systematically down all the tight-printed columns of Ks.

'Perhaps it begins with a C,' I said, and started again there.

'No it doesn't. It can't. I know.'

'How do you know? You don't know German.'

Conico, Conimbriga, Coningsby, Coniston. He was right. It just wasn't there.

'See.'

I went home just briefly that day from the Laceys'.
It was late in the afternoon. It was beginning to get dark and there were lights on in the house.

'Somebody's there. Who's there?' When I saw the lights in the windows I knew that I didn't want anyone with me, not Mrs Lacey, not Susan, no one who had any words to them. I wanted to go in on my own, like always.

'It's only the piano tuner.'

I could hear the piano soon as the door was open: a note repeated, adjusted, played again.

'Why's the piano tuner here?'

To tune the piano, said Mrs Lacey, nothing strange about it. There was no point in sending the man away once he had made the journey. So she had told Margaret to let him in.

We had come only to pack a bag. My father was coming home with Peter and then we were going away for a few days. He would be driving right now, fetching Peter from school.

When we went upstairs to my room the sound was there too.

'What shall I take?'

The notes were insistent, distorting, dragging on the ear. I never liked the piano tuner coming. He made the world go out of shape.

'You're going to the sea,' Susan said.

When the piano tuner finished we saw him go before we turned off the lights, and Mrs Lacey double-locked all the doors. Later that same evening my father came and we drove away in the dark.

I slept in the car. A transient security in sleeping on a journey, in being carried through the night, and when the motion stopped, being lifted, wrapped and still curled, and knowing that you were somewhere else and yet not having to open your eyes, and being safe and put into bed. When I woke the sea was there before me. I drew back the plaid-patterned curtains from a big window, and saw the sea in a straight line in front of the house. There were two beds in the room and Peter was still asleep in the other one. It was the room of some boy or boys who we did not know; school photographs of strangers on the chest of drawers and a dartboard on the wall.

The sea was a dull pencil colour with white edges against the shore. I had never come to the seaside in winter before. It looked so cold, wide and silent beyond the fastened window. I did not hear it until I went out,

soon as breakfast was over. I ran ahead of Peter, down the
steps from the garden on to the narrow strip of the beach,
and low waves came in and foamed at my feet, and I ran
along that beach and over the wooden groin and along the
next, until I came to a fence and a line of bare and tattered
trees. I stood there and looked across the sea to the long
smooth outline of an island. It was clear that it was an
island because I could see each end of it, and the sea
between was still grey, but scaly now that the sun had
broken through to shine on it.

We stayed four or five days, long enough to learn that
the island was the Isle of Wight and that the rocks that
stood out in the sea beyond its tip were called the Needles,
though they seemed too thick and solid for such a name.
The house belonged to some people that my father said he
had known before, before the war and before my mother,
but I did not remember ever having heard of them. Henry
and Madeleine, they were called. He never said which one
of them was his friend, which one had known him first;
only that they were kind and that their own children were
away at school. I learnt to play darts and Peter shot a bow
and arrows, and we played ping-pong on a table in the
garage. One of the days my father and Henry went
somewhere dressed in suits, and we children were left
with Madeleine alone. Madeleine took us out for a walk
with her two red setters that bounded with streaming hair
along the shore.

*   *   *

'Will we go there again, Daddy?'

'What, to Madeleine's?'

'I liked it there. I want to go in the summer so I can go in the sea.'

'Perhaps,' he said. 'If they ask us.'

We never did. There was no sequential reality to add to this interlude, which came to memory later in disconnected images like snapshots or a dream. Later, I was to wonder who Henry and Madeleine were, and if they really did exist, and told myself that I would surely find them if only I were to go along the south coast, to sail say from Bournemouth to Southampton, and look in along all the shore with the Isle of Wight behind me. Henry and Madeleine I would not know again; they seemed quite indistinct; but I was certain that I would recognise the house. A safe house. I had the image of it clear: set just back from the beach, not old, probably Thirties, white, parts of the upper storey hung with tiles; wide windows and dormers in the roof above; all looking out to the sea. And hydrangeas. I had an image of them by the steps that led up from the sand, steps made of broad planks with pale sand scattered across them, and tall blue hydrangea bushes. Yet remembering it afterwards, it seems impossible that it could have been so: if we visited the place just that one time in January, then how could I have known the colour of the flowers?

So little that is known for sure, so much confused. The past seems sometimes mutable as the present, changing before my eyes. I had to learn to fix it about a constant, at least something near a constant. The house we lived in, that was fixed. Every piece of it I used to go over and fix about myself. For years I did this, when I was at school and again later, in other places after I had moved away. I would take myself around the house and the garden in my mind before I went to sleep: into the hall, through open doors and up the stairs and around the upstairs rooms.

To my own room, with a picture of a rider on the wall and the tiny glass animals that I collected on the shelves. Peter's room, my father's with the yellow bedspread, the spare room that was just that, spare, with white airy emptiness, the little room where the ironing was done that had a round window where I used to hide away and read.

Downstairs then, and out of the French windows into the garden.

When we got home it was just the three of us. The house told us that, it was so clean and neat; the letters on the sideboard in the hall, all the loose papers and magazines in piles at the corners of the tables. Margaret must have come every day even though we were gone, polished the furniture and the silver and the brass handles on the doors, and left the smell of it behind her. Tidied and hoovered and dusted and polished, and erased. Something had been erased from the house, and so completely that I did not see at first that it was the presence of my mother. Her coat gone from its hook and with it her shoes, the fur-lined boots that she wore to go out in the cold. Her bag and her diary that she kept in the kitchen. Jars and bottles from the bathroom. From every room, her touch: the arrangements of things, the positions of cushions and ashtrays; the sense that she had been there.

Yet this was more than Margaret could have done alone. I knew that someone must have been there with her, if not my father then Mrs Lacey or someone other who was strange to me. Some cold hands had been through and touched everything, systematically identifying, selecting things, taking out her clothes with the soft smell to them, lifting them up, folding them away, clearing her dressing table, gathering up the lipsticks and the nail polish and the cotton wool and the compacts, disposing of them, while Margaret went stolidly after and breathed on the glass and cleaned away the rings where the little bottles had stood and the spilled powder.

Sometimes when I made a mistake in my schoolwork, my mother used to help rub it out. When I did it myself I left a shadow on the page, and sometimes crumpled it or took the surface off the paper. When my mother did it she held the page smooth between red-varnished fingertips and rubbed so gently with the other hand that, if the pencil had not been pressed too hard, the paper was left white and perfect and good as if it was never written on.

The house was like that. There were no marks. You had to make an effort to remember where she had been.

They had rubbed her out.

The strange thing was that the space which spoke her absence most was not any of the rooms she had lived in, not her bedroom even with her dressing table by the window and the stool before it, none of these but my own room. Only there was there a sense of her, pressing in. She was in the walls, the curtains, in the dark slit where the cupboard door failed to close. There, or about to be there, known, immanent, her voice most of all, about to break through, almost recalled, so that I almost heard its tone, its warmth, its accent. And yet the silence held and there were no words. It held and quivered, like a note sung too long, until I felt that I could not breathe. I ran, gasping, to my father's room. See: my mother's room had already become my father's room. There was his bed and there was space in it. The sheets in the space were cold, but warm close up to him. A little later Peter came in too, and the other side warmed also.

I have never come to Berlin before. In forty years I somehow never found the time.

Peter came here as soon as he began to travel, a hunched student on a rail pass, and when he got home he spoke of the divided city's scars and its lack of beauty yet he seemed to have preferred it to Paris or Amsterdam or Rome. He was drawn back repeatedly in those years and again later, after the Wall came down. He made an effort to come and see me just after that, invited himself for a weekend as he had not done in years and brought me what he said was a piece of the Wall as a present. (And that was just what it was, a chunk of graffitied concrete, and I have no idea where it has got to. Perhaps my husband has thrown it away by now. My husband is a tidy man and has no place for what has no function.)

'I don't know what you expect to find,' my husband said when I told him I was planning this trip. 'It was all a very long time ago.'

*   *   *

38

It takes getting used to, travelling alone. Life seems at some moments blank, as there is no one to share it with, and at others strangely vivid. Being without habit, husband, family becomes all at once like being without a skin, senses bared to every impression, to the sunlight, the morning, the bus ride from the airport, the confusion of catching a tram, buying and punching a ticket in a place where you do not speak the language. At least the hotel was not hard to find. I checked in and took up my case but did not unpack it and only sat there for a while on the bed. It is a tolerable room, more spacious than I might have expected, and it smells fresh. I have taken the bed closest to the window. The other one by the wall I will leave untouched. If it is clear that I have not used it then perhaps they will not have the bother of changing the sheets.

I shall leave sightseeing for tomorrow. It is lucky that the route of the bus from the airport passed by so many of the famous sites. I have at least glimpsed the new dome of the Reichstag, the Brandenburg Gate, Unter den Linden, Alexanderplatz. I know where these things are.

This first evening I thought I should stick to the streets by the hotel. I walked until I came to a triangular platz with trees and cafés about it. No one was sitting at the tables outside as there was a biting wind. The cold was getting to me even as I was walking, but with so many cafés and restaurants it was hard to choose where to stop. It was some time later that I found this one, a place much like any other with a menu board outside on the pavement, but a couple were just leaving, and the door they held open seemed like an invitation. The restaurant is cosy and there is white linen on the table, and lentil soup.

I have a book to read. Isn't that what lone women are supposed to do when they travel: read books propped open with knives at restaurant tables? *The Meaning of Treason* by Rebecca West, the 1965 edition updated with chapters on the spy cases of the Sixties: Philby, Burgess and Maclean, Blake, Vassall, Profumo, the Portland Ring. I particularly mean to read the chapters about the Portland case, about Houghton and Gee and Lonsdale and the Krogers. I shall not begin to read it with concentration until later when I am back in the hotel room. Here in the restaurant the book is just for cover.

I t was the story of the Krogers that people were to
remember long after everything else about Portland
was forgotten. Houghton and Gee were understandable if
despicable. Lonsdale was a Russian and a professional. The
secrets they traded became obsolete. The Krogers remained an enigma.

What was interesting about them was the completeness
of the lie they lived. In person, they entirely convinced.
They seemed perfectly nice, middle class, trustworthy,
classifiable, the sort of people others liked: Helen and
Peter, the nice New Zealand couple, who had seemed to fit
in so easily to suburban living. British people rather
expected that of New Zealanders, back then. New Zealanders were provincial in that special Commonwealth way;
you trusted them almost more than your own people
because places like New Zealand and Canada were thinly
populated and a little behind the times, and kept to the old
values that reminded you how good it was to be British.

It was only when they were gone, when the police had
taken them away, the evening of that same Saturday in

41

January when the other three were arrested at Waterloo, that the things they left behind revealed who they really were.

Their house was a bungalow on a suburban street in Ruislip, a house of such a common design, with its twinned bow windows and white cement, and brick edging to the porch, that anyone who passed it might think they could reasonably guess at the life that went on inside. It looked as predictable as a mass-produced doll's house, to which a child might add pieces bought in little packs, all made to scale, all with the safety in them of standardised design: a sofa for the lounge, a coffee table with a Ronson lighter on it, a Murphy radiogram, a bookcase, a bathroom suite, a kitchen cabinet with two drawers in the middle. At six-thirty on a wintry Saturday evening the lights should be on, and figures placed upon the sofa, *Dixon of Dock Green* on television – a scene to be glimpsed perhaps through the gap in the not-quite-yet-closed curtains.

So it appeared, and yet it was not so.

The Murphy radiogram had headphones fitted and concealed in its back, and was tuned to a high frequency band for the reception of foreign transmissions.

The Ronson table lighter had a concealed cavity in its base containing negative films with dates and signal plans for wireless communications with call signs based on the names of Russian towns and rivers.

The Bible in the bookcase contained pieces of light-sensitised cellophane to be used for the making of micro-dots.

The tin of Three Flowers talcum powder in the bathroom sprinkled talc only from a central compartment and concealed a microdot reader in secret compartments alongside.

Hidden in the bedroom were a box holding a microscope and glass slides, a magazine of 35mm film concealed beneath a chest of drawers, an extraordinary length of electric flex, thousands of US dollars. Elsewhere were cameras, tape recorders, photographic developing materials, black-out screens for the conversion of bathroom into darkroom.

Beneath a trap door under the kitchen fridge was a makeshift cache containing more dollars, more lenses and cameras, including reducing lenses for making microdots, and a transmitter with a foreign plug.

And in the attic space among Helen's carefully stored overwintering apples – stored on slats so they could breathe, no one of them touching another, the smell of them sweet and domestic beneath the roof – was a radio aerial seventy-four foot nine inches long.

Tools, gadgets, evidence. That is what fascinated people so. There was the ordinariness of the people and then there was the evidence of the house, like an extraordinary game of Cluedo.

That nice friendly middle-class woman Helen, who always has a smile for her neighbours, a bone for the dog or a present for the children, who will do errands for you or bring you fresh eggs from the local farm, connects the aerial in the roof to the transmitter beneath the kitchen floor, using the flex that was found in the bedroom, puts to her head the earphones that were concealed in the back of the radiogram, tunes in, calls *Volga ya Azov*, or *Lena ya Amur*, transmits to Moscow.

Their names are Morris and Lona or Leontina Cohen. They are Americans, not New Zealanders, Communists and associates of the Rosenbergs. In 1950 when the Rosenbergs were arrested the Cohens had dropped out of sight, and somehow, somewhere, in some Soviet country, in the time between then and the time when they arrived in England in 1955, they had acquired the skills to run their own spy cell, learnt radio operation and the making of microdots, learnt to set up a convincing cover as antiquarian booksellers, learnt to be the Krogers.

How did it feel to do that? Perhaps it was easier than it seemed. Perhaps you simply took up the role and smiled in it. You walked out and went to the shops in it, and gradually you became it or it became you.

Or you wake in a hotel room in a distant city and shake off the sleep and remember, this is who you will be, and dress and go down the stairs and make yourself whoever it is as you eat your foreign breakfast.

Perhaps it began to happen with the first response from the outside, the trust of a stranger, the first making of a friend. And what then? After a day, a week, a year, a life set up as someone else? Who were you then? Who were the Cohens, or Krogers, when they were alone? Who were they to each other? Was Peter Kroger the same man all through as Morris Cohen, the Bronx boy who won a sports scholarship to the University of Mississippi? He had kept Cohen's fitness and physique, an enthusiasm for sport that had transmuted into a love of cricket, and presumably Cohen had shared the same easy charm, though his hair had not been such a distinguished grey. And Helen? When the case was over it was known that Helen was Lona but that was even harder for those who had thought themselves their friends to accept, for Helen had seemed so convincingly and warmly herself. Perhaps the different passports stood for nothing and she was one person after all, and a friend of Leontina Petka as she had been, the daughter of Polish immigrants to America, would be equally a friend of Helen the New Zealand housewife?

I put down room key and guidebook on a table and go and dither before the hotel buffet. Other guests nod to me as I pass. Perhaps they guess that I am English. I can be whatever woman they see. I nod back, knowing they know nothing of who I am inside.

There was a suggestion that the deception was hard for Helen. It came out in the course of the trial that people remembered her from the time when the Krogers had lived in Catford, before they moved to the bungalow at Ruislip. Women neighbours saw that she used to cry a lot. She would cry alone in the house and when she came out her eyes would show it. They assumed, knowing (as they

45

thought) the sort of person she was, that the sadness in her life was that the couple had no children. It was a flaw in the Helen Kroger story, the thing that neighbours noted, and talked about, and pitied her for: the lack of the thing that rooted a woman, gave her purpose in that suburban daytime world.

Yet why did she have no children? Was that too a part of the job?

The woman who spoke in court never once appeared to diverge from character. She may have converted the bathroom in the Ruislip bungalow into a temporary dark-room for the developing of photographs and the making of microdots, but when she spoke she spoke as a housewife, so normal, so true to type, that other women who heard her could not help feeling that she was one of them. She liked the man Lonsdale, she said, Lonsdale who was arrested two hours before her at Waterloo, because he was helpful in the house. He brought in coal and helped her with the washing up, and sometimes he helped her with her hobby of photography. It rang true. Peter Kroger, by the sound of him, probably spent his Sundays doing the crossword or watching the cricket or deep in his books. Who wouldn't have appreciated a charming younger man like that as a weekend guest? It made spying such a homely sort of a thing.

Then there was the moment of her arrest, when Helen had asked one favour before leaving the house: 'As I am going out for some time may I go and stoke the boiler in the kitchen?' She spoke in character, even then, and the only oddity of it was that she picked up her handbag to take with her – and whenever did a woman take her handbag when she went to stoke the boiler? When Superintendent Smith took it from her he found in it an envelope full of codes and rendezvous points and microdots.

G odfrey Lacey swore when he saw the arrest of the
Portland spies announced on the News that Monday.
I noticed it because usually Mr Lacey was not a vehement
man. He had the erectness to him of a former soldier but
not the authority; his words hesitant, his eyes never quite
direct, his moustache the most emphatic point on his face.
But at this moment the anger in him was visible. He swore
again, never mind that Susan and I were in the room nor
that his wife was trying to get his attention. He took up his
gin and swallowed, and I saw the chill disgust those of his
generation felt for spies and traitors.

Just as he spoke the second time, Daphne called again
from the hall. Though she had a voice that could be
piercing, he did not seem to hear it. She held her hand
over the receiver and called him, then when he did not
come she returned to the conversation she was having. She
was standing at the table in the hall where the telephone
was kept. The telephone was for information still in those
days, not a social instrument, and was kept in the hall
without even a chair beside it.

I remember the simultaneous occurrences: Godfrey swearing, the television, the gin glass taken up from the Burmese side table, Daphne on the telephone, Susan and myself playing cards. It was as if some some electrical event had occurred, a charged moment, and each random piece of it was crystallised. Yet the meaning of each piece was not initially clear, or if any one were dependent upon the others. At first the Portland case, and Godfrey's anger, seemed to be no more than a part of the adult background, something to be absorbed vaguely like other news stories, like the Congo, like Algeria, like Macmillan or de Gaulle, so many names and places that my father and the Laceys and their friends and my friends' parents turned about.

It was Peter who made the connection. Peter's fault then. Peter who was so clever but did not know where you divided stories from reality.

A year on. Again, summer. Loose days. Open doors and windows.

Peter's school broke up before mine did. He was at home for a week, more, on his own. I do not know what he got up to. I suppose that he stayed in his room, brooded, read, made models, watched the cricket, went next door for lunch, did what he always did at home, and that it did not make much difference to him if anyone else was there or not.

There was a Test match. When the Test match was on the curtains in the sitting room were drawn when I came home from school and there were men in white on the screen and a lull of voices and he sat rapt and might as well have not been there at all. Then it was over, or rained off, and he read a book about spies. He had progressed from war to spies.

'Look at these dates, Anna, in my book.'

It was a book that he had been given, a big book with a glossy cover and black-and-white photographs in it like those in the newspapers.

'That's just after my birthday.'

'Not only that.' Peter was so insistent, always getting cross. 'Not just the day, silly. The year as well.'

'Of course, I know. I knew that all along. It's just before Mummy died, isn't it?' The words were big, when I spoke them. I think I may not ever have spoken them before.

'That's it, exactly, that's the point.'

I did not see why he was so excited. A day in January, two days before that day, some people arrested, men and women. Snapshots of them smiling, looking like anyone else. Like people we might know, not criminals.

'So what?'

'Don't you see? The arrests were made on Saturday evening. It wasn't in the news until Monday. She would have found out, seen the headlines when she got to Oxford or heard it somewhere on the way. Maybe she heard it on the radio.'

'What's it got to do with her anyway?'

He looked at me as if I was a fool, not seeing that events must have a cause. In Peter's world a thing did not just come out of nowhere. There must be before and after, reasons why.

'Did she crash on the way there or on the way back? Did they tell you?'

'I don't know.'

I had always thought it happened in the morning. It happened in the fog, on the way. The car went off with its red lights fading into the fog and it happened on an empty hill somewhere, just the car and the fog, and black ice. I had not thought that it could be anything but that. Now I saw that it might have happened anywhere – on the main road, in the traffic, in the afternoon.

'Think. We should know. It might be important.'

'Well, we just don't.'

Daphne Lacey is calling from the phone.

'Darling!'

Godfrey is not listening to her. His eyes are still on the screen.

'Come here a minute. There's something I have to say to you.'

We are playing beggar-my-neighbour. Susan turns up a king, wins three; a jack, wins one, and with it the pack.

'Buggers!' says Godfrey Lacey, and it is not clear now whether this relates to the news story or the fact that his wife is calling him. The man on the television is saying that five persons have been charged under Section One of the Official Secrets Act and are being held at Bow Street Police Station.

'Buggers,' he says again.

51

The television moves on to the weather, unwatched, as Godfrey Lacey crosses the hall and goes into the kitchen and closes the door. A band of high pressure reaching the west by morning. The fog clearing overnight. Frost and a clear day to follow.

'I don't know, Peter. I don't know anything!'

I screamed at him. I didn't even know that I was about to scream. I screamed so loud that if someone else, some adult, had been in the house they would have come running as to danger, then when they saw that there was no physical danger things might have been said, an explanation given, and just possibly it might all have stopped there, right then at the beginning. But there was no one save our two selves to hear.

'I don't know anything and anyway it doesn't matter. None of it matters. None of this means anything. It wasn't as if she knew those people or anything.'

Whatever else Peter knew about it either he was pretending or he wasn't going to tell. He was fixed back in his book.

'How can you be so sure?'

It must have been after that day that we began to watch. Or perhaps it was not. Perhaps it did not begin at any point. Perhaps we had always watched, as children always have, watched our adults; children wide-eyed, the adults like to think, but seeing so much more than the adults could or would like to know.

We had always watched but we became conscious of it only once we began to think that there was something to be discovered, some secret or some story there. From that moment on the watching became deliberate, more intense.

MI5 kept the Krogers' house under surveillance for two months before their arrest. Each day agents came to the house of some neighbours just over the road, where there was a bedroom with a window at the side overlooking their frontage. The agents were women generally, since the visits of women were less likely to be remarked upon in a district where husbands went to work and wives had coffee and arranged charity collections and events at the local arts society. Mrs Search, who lived in the surveillance house, considered herself a friend of Helen Kroger's and continued to see her and have her to visit throughout this period. It was revealed later that she found the experience deeply troubling.

There was no one I watched more closely than my father. In those days I was aware of him sometimes as if my nerves reached into him and felt his moods – his occasional pleasure, his sadness, his irritations – from the inside.

Alec Wyatt. Linguist, speaker of five European languages. He was ten years older than my mother and he used be a teacher. Then when the war came he was too short-sighted to be a proper soldier so he had done something in codes instead, sitting at a desk with a pencil in his hand. Peter was ashamed of that, the idea that his father had chewed a pencil all through the war. Even if he had been to places that sounded good, like Baghdad, and Italy, and Berlin.

When I started a diary I wrote what I had done and thought each day on the correct dated page. I kept the blank undated pages at the back for other people. I wrote notes on how they looked and what they did. The diary was a stiff book with embossed gold lettering, *My Diary 1962* on the front, and a lock to keep it private. I must have kept it up for half the year, and then tired of it, or left it somewhere, and never wrote in it again.

The first description was of my father. Fairish hair, a little bit grey. Grey-blue eyes, soft behind the glasses. Tall. I thought how I would describe him if I was a stranger and put 'a little woolly but kind'. I set myself to observing his actions, his movement, his face. When I grew up there was proof of the closeness of my observation in the fact that I seemed to know how to garden soon as I had a garden of my own. The tasks were familiar as if I had always performed them, and my fingers knew as if they had always done it how to plant seeds, how to sprinkle the compost, thin, plug out, how to hold the secateurs and at which bud to prune the roses, though I could never recall having been taught these things or done them before, but only that I had watched them done. Almost better than his face I could recall his hands, his fingers dirty with soil, unusually broad thumbs, distinctive so that I would have recognised them anywhere.

At any time I supposed that I might have asked him what we needed to know. I might have asked him most easily when he was gardening, when I was standing close by and he was working and it was easy between us, his hand on the fork, the tines breaking the soil, the fresh green weeds falling back on to it. There were so many questions a child could ask her father at a time like that.

Why does the Queen say 'we' instead of 'I'?

Which way up does a pineapple grow?

What is a mushroom cloud?

I might have asked about Königsberg, and I might as easily, almost as easily, have asked if he or Mummy knew the Portland people. He worked for the Government anyway, we knew that, speaking languages; and there was something secret in it so he might reasonably have known some spies. Yet I did not ask. I stood by and I learnt only the root forms of weeds: how white and brittle were the roots of bindweed, which broke when you pulled them and left bits that grew again from deeper down than you could dig, or the red hairy obscenity of nettle roots that snaked this way and that just beneath the surface of the soil. And when he straightened himself and rested he smiled and ruffled my hair, and I was happy then that I had not spoken.

One day when he was gardening Susan came round and we played at dressing up. We must have been nine or ten by then, and we didn't dress up so much. We had used to do it often when we were smaller. Sometimes my mother would help, fixing our hair and tying turbans and sashes, making us into witches and princesses and sultans with fine moustaches that she drew with a burnt cork. Now we did it all ourselves. Because we were older we did not dress as make-believe figures any more but as the women we might become.

Susan had brought over a dress that she said came from Malaya. It was a flimsy thing of lime-green silk. In Malaya her parents drank cocktails and went to parties. She said that the parties went on late into the night and the moon was bigger than in England and the nights were hot. The spaghetti straps and low-cut bodice showed up the paleness of her skin and her gawky body's lack of form, yet the dress, the idea and the colour of it, made her bold. Susan was normally quiet and self-effacing, pale, freckled, red-haired, always a little stooped with shyness, yet all of a sudden she put up her hair and strutted like an actress and became a flattened version of her mother.

'Don't laugh. What are you laughing at?'

'You look funny, that's all.'

'There's another one you can wear. Mummy said I could borrow it too.'

'No. There's something else. I know where it is.'

We went to my father's room. He was outside, mowing the lawn. I had just heard the mower start up. He wouldn't come in before tea.

In the wardrobe, at the very back of the wardrobe behind all of his clothes, was a dress. It had been left behind when everything else was cleared. Whoever it was that cleared the house had by intention or error left me that one dress, zipped up in a bag as it had come from the dry-cleaner's. There was that dress and there was her fur jacket, and a drawer of folded silk scarves and her jewellery in a velvet-lined box. The dress was a very dark blue, not so glamorous as Susan's, but I had a notion that I had seen my mother in it, once for some distant occasion. I took off my clothes and put it on, there in my father's room before the tall mahogany wardrobe, and then took out the fur on its silk-covered hanger.

'It's silver fox,' I said. 'It came from Berlin. Daddy bought it on the black market.'

'Did your mother wear it?'

'Of course she did. She wore it when she went to the theatre.'

Yet I had never seen it worn, never seen my mother go to the theatre.

It was soft as Susan's cat, though the silver-tipped fur was longer, and it carried a scent that must have once been hers. Putting it on, feeling its weight and the coolness of the satin lining, was like slipping into water.

'You look like a film star.'

Susan had brought high-heeled shoes, too big. My mother's feet were smaller but all her shoes were gone. The shoes made us tall and the make-up we had put on made us old. We saw ourselves in the long mirror: a redhead, a blonde, red-lipped, high-heeled, lime green and fur and midnight blue. Susan stuffed her bodice with socks, pouted, posed. I stood in the slender mirror space beside her in the fox jacket and the dark-blue dress, and wondered if anyone could have said then that I too had a look of my mother, if not in my colouring then in the way I stood or smiled, or held my hand out to take an imaginary cigarette.

'You look lovely, darling,' said Susan, and proffered an imaginary case.

I mimed the taking of one and Susan lit it, saw the curls of smoke rising between us as Susan snapped the case shut.

'They're Russian,' Susan said. 'I always smoke Russian.'

We had glasses in our hands with cherries on sticks, raised them to our cherry lips.

*   *   *

I was not sure, afterwards, if that was the first moment that my father caught sight of us, or if he had been looking already for some time. Yet the intensity of his look struck suddenly like a blow.

The glasses were gone, our hands empty. We were children again, dressed like tarts in our mothers' clothes, and he was angry. His stare went to me, to Susan, back again to me. I thought that he would shout. I would have hated to hear him shout.

His voice when it came was soft.

'Take those things off. Right away.'

Once we would have, but we were older now. We were shy to undress in front of him. We stood, frozen in our dresses and our lipstick, and he looked at us as if we were ghosts. I saw that his hand had blood on it, his finger wrapped in a bloodied handkerchief. He had cut himself and come to fetch a plaster from the bathroom. He looked at us that one moment and then went on.

Later, when Susan had gone, he came in from the garden again and scrubbed the soil from his hands, and asked if I had put the clothes away.

'That's right,' he said. 'That's a good girl. And once things are put away they are best left that way. No need to take them out again, is there, poppet?'

*   *   *

'We can't ask Daddy. Not anything. He doesn't want to talk about it,' I said to Peter after that.

'Even if you ask him? You're always asking him things.'

'No,' I said. 'He doesn't want to be reminded.'

We went away that second summer to France. 'We'll go to the Brittany coast,' my father said. 'You said you wanted to go to the sea.' We went there on a ferry, and the sea was grey. I stood against the rail at the stern and watched the white V of the wake drawing away from England, and the gulls following in it. It was the first time I had been abroad.

I wrote in my diary that it rained in France. We drove down straight roads through grey sheets of rain. We came to long beaches and walked the tiring length of them in the sand to look at rusting tanks and debris from the war. The beaches had beautiful names, Arromanches, Omaha, Utah. This was where the Allies landed, my father said, tens of thousands of soldiers jumping into the cold waves off flat-bottomed boats with their guns held over their heads. He and Peter looked at everything, the machines, the signs, the maps, the photographs in the museums. I watched the waves and made tracks in the sand. Where the sand was wet and shiny close to the sea's edge, my footprints disappeared as if they were sucked away.

When we swam the water was cold. The beach was shallow so that we had to walk out a long way until it came to our waists and we could swim. There must be bits there, I wrote, on the sand where you cannot see it beneath the water. If there are bits on the beaches they must be in the sea as well. Things from the war. Guns, helmets, bodies. Soldiers who were killed. As soon as the water was deep enough, I swam and tried not to touch the ground again. Once or twice I swam out to where I could feel a pull on my legs, pulling me out, away, down the beach from where I'd begun. My father called me back, then came quickly and swam out. He said it was a current of water that pulled at me. It had a name, the undertow. It was the bottom of the wave going back out to sea.

I wrote about it in my diary. How there must be Americans down there beneath the sea. In the hotel where we stayed the sugar came in little printed packets with pictures of the beaches on them. I collected all the different ones I could find and stuck them in the book, and the tickets from the places we visited.

'What are you doing?' asked Peter.

'Making a record. So I can remember it all after.'

Peter played with the other English boys at the hotel. There were three of them, a noisy family whose presence dominated the restaurant at supper, laughing, shouting, spilling things. They were rowdy boys and I did not like them. I felt sorry for the old man who had the table next to them and who sipped his coffee in the mornings from his teaspoon. Poor Monsieur Alphonse, I wrote, giving him the name, knowing that Alphonse was a French name. He was a thin man and wore a hat whenever he went out so that his face was pale as paper. Once the boys let me join them on a raid to the kitchens, and we went down in the lift to the basement and sneaked around until a waiter chased us out, and everything was white and shining steel. On the way back up to our rooms Monsieur Alphonse got in, and we all laughed fit I thought to deafen him.

'Where's your mother?' asked one of the boys. Their mother was always in the lounge, in a chair at the window writing postcards and looking out to sea.

'She's a spy,' said Peter, 'working undercover.'

I was glad he did not say that she was dead.

When I was older and looked over the photographs I realised how difficult the trip must have been for my father. He read his books and saw all the beaches but it rained and we complained that we didn't like the food.

The weather changed just before we were due to leave. Soon as I woke that last morning I knew how good the day was even before the curtains were open. The sky was bright and the sea was shining under the sun. We went into the town and bought lunch, a long golden loaf of bread, cheese, tomatoes, peaches, and drove out a long way along the coast. The road seemed to ride the coast, up and down, with views coming and going of the sea. Then we stopped and walked, out along a strip of sand with the sea on either side, to a rocky point, and there we had our picnic, where there was no one else and only a view with nothing between us and America. I remember how I bored my eyes into the horizon as if I might see it, if I were to look hard enough. Where those soldiers came from. How far was it? How long did it take to float there? Had the undertow by now taken them home?

It was hours later when we walked back, and the tide had come in and covered over a section of the causeway.

'Alec,' my mother would have said. My mother had a special way of saying Alec, an inflexion no one else ever used. 'So clever, but always so impractical.'

The stretch of sea where the causeway had been was like all the rest of the sea, nothing to distinguish where the land lay beneath. It was not wide but it was growing, as the waves lapped up to where we stood. My father took the blanket I was carrying, rolled it tighter and crammed it into the bag with the picnic things. Follow me. And tentatively the three of us started to walk into the water, and I saw us as we walked, the tall man leading, treading delicately, feeling for ground, the girl behind and then the boy.

The water was alive, rushing in. It reached up my legs and above my waist.

'I can't, Daddy.'

And all three turned and went back.

Then the boy was left on what was now the island, and the man began to cross again carrying the girl on his shoulders.

The water came to his chest, over my feet as he carried me. I looked back. Peter was left on the island. The sea was washing against it, rising towards him, making the distance longer, the distance stretching in both directions as we walked away.

'When the tide comes in, it doesn't all go under, does it?'

'No, I'm sure not. There are grasses there.'

Then the water was lower and we were coming out of it. He put me down and went back for Peter. I was alone now, on the mainland, and he was in the stretching water and Peter was on the island. There was an interval of time when each of us was separated from the other by the moving water, and I saw that was how we were, the three of us, each separated, surrounded by a dark sea that moved across and covered over the ground. But then he came up out of it, on to the dunes and the grass, up to Peter where he stood, so still, and he turned, and Peter climbed on to his back.

He carried Peter across piggy-back, and Peter carried the picnic bag high so that it was above the level of the water.

At dinner that evening I felt bold. I suppose that it was because of the day, because of the sunshine and because of our adventure, because it was our last day also.

'Where Mummy went to the seaside, was it like this?'

'That would have been in Germany. The Baltic. It's a very different sea.'

We were eating crabs. The hotel kept serving up crab. I didn't mind the meat but I didn't know how to get it out so he was breaking the claws for me and putting what was edible on my plate. He was not looking at me as he spoke but focused on the claw in his hands, and his answer was precise and yet it quite deflected the question.

'This is the Atlantic Ocean. The Baltic is just a sea hemmed around by countries. It only connects to the ocean by a narrow sound. There's hardly a tide. And the water's different even, with much less salt in it than other seawater because of all the rivers that empty into it.'

'What does that mean?' asked Peter.

'It's almost like fresh water. Lovely to swim in even if it's cold.'

A dark sea like a lake. People in it, swimming, floating. There was a picture of the place where she went at my piano teacher's house, a photograph on the mantelpiece, but the picture was just of people on the beach there, and you had to imagine the sea in the distance.

'Mrs Cahn has a picture of it.'

'Of what?'

'Where Mummy went.'

'Did she go there too?'

'They talked about it once.'

'Some of those Baltic resorts were very popular. Still are, probably, though I don't know now.'

Then Peter butted in.

'Mrs Cahn's Jewish.'

'No, she's not,' I said. 'She's German. She came here from Germany.'

'That's right. She's Jewish and German. Both.' And a moment later he said, just for the hell of it, just because he was Peter, 'Do you know what happened to the Jews who stayed in Germany, the ones who didn't leave like she did?'

'What?'

'The Germans killed them all. They stuffed them into chambers one on top of the other and gassed them and made them into soap.'

My father was saying, 'Peter, there's no need for that.'

'Well, it's true.'

'That's enough.'

I could see the 'but' beginning to form on Peter's lips. It did not come out. My father stopped him. He slammed his hand with the crab claw in it down on the napkin, so hard that the glasses shook. He did not speak again but only looked Peter in the eye.

Silly Peter. Anyone knew that soap wasn't made out of people.

There were so many things that adults did not seem to see, even when they heard them spoken, even when they were there before their eyes. There were things I saw that my father did not see. I went out for walks with him, that summer when we were home. It did not rain when we were home. Possibly it had not rained, he said, it had rained hardly at all, for all the time that we were away in France, since the lawn when we came back had barely grown and the ground was very hard. We walked through the fields on the edge of the village where the wheat had just been harvested, down tracks through the stubble, and I saw between the golden stalks where the soil had dried and cracked. I thought of what I knew about earthquakes and it seemed to me then that each crack showed where a chasm might open beneath our feet, but my father walked on, his dry hand holding mine lightly when I reached for it, unaware of any danger. He did not see that the hard harvest land was dead land, cracking open. He did not see that in Peter also there were cracks.

*   *   *

'J. Edgar Hoover says the Communists have three hundred thousand spies hiding all over the West. That's a whole secret army, everywhere.'

'Who's J. Edgar Hoover?'

'He's the head of the FBI. In America.'

That was the sort of thing Peter talked about. The FBI and MI5 and Moscow Centre. He didn't talk about normal things. I wrote that in my book. I wrote that he was thin and that his hair fell across his face, probably because he was always looking down, at a model or a book, looking at the ground, looking away. (That's how he is in the photographs I have; he's looking the wrong way or he has a hand across his face at the wrong moment, or he's squinting because of the sun.) I understood him because he was my brother but still he was strange to me. He was clever. Everybody said he was clever. He read fast, he remembered facts and figures, and could repeat them to you any time. But there were other things, simple things, that he didn't seem to see at all, as if facts were easier for him than reality.

His books told him whatever could be known about the various secret services: where their offices were located, how they were run, the hierarchies and procedures. He drew a diagram to show me how spy rings were organised. He said that Moscow Centre excelled at this. There was the director of operations at the heart of it all, and then separate arms reaching out, like a spider, but there could be an infinite number of arms stretching a great distance, sometimes with one, two or three joints away from the central body. At the tip of each arm was the field operative, and at each joint a liaison agent, and the operative knew no one but the agent, neither the director nor any of the other operatives in the ring. Sometimes the operative never even met the liaison, but communicated by messages at pre-fixed drops or by radio signals. All the messages were coded and recoded. Each operative had one code name in the field and another code name at the centre. No one knew more than it was absolutely necessary for them to know, so no one could tell. So every operative was separate, in his own cell, and yet the whole thing was also like a spider's web, and when something touched it, the vibrations ran all through but only the one operative might be affected; and if that operative was captured or something, then that operation could be wrapped up and left, quite separate from the rest.

'Don't they save them?' I asked.

'It's more important to save the system.'

He said that we should have our own code, so that when he went away to school nobody could read our letters.

'But you don't write me letters. You always write to Daddy, not to me.'

'But if I did, if I needed to, we'd have the code. We've got to have the code first.'

Such urgency in the way he talked, head down, eyes moving on before I could catch them.

'Can't I just write ordinary writing?'

'Of course you can, for ordinary things. The code's for emergencies.'

He said we would have some words for a key. I must remember these words, and then I would put the letters of the alphabet beside them and switch them, in order, cutting out the ones that repeated, and switch the letters when I wrote. He didn't like any of the phrases I suggested so he gave me his own, Winston Churchill. Where Churchill ended, the code continued, the alphabet running on in the usual way. If people didn't know where we'd started from, they'd never work it out.

'You'll have to write it down each time, and destroy the paper after so no one can find it.'

He made me practise it and write him notes so that I had it straight before he went away, message after message encrypted, folded and double-folded and slipped into a pocket or left beneath a cereal bowl. *Can you read this? If you can, put an orange in the fridge. Watch Margaret till she goes then come and find me.* It got easier as you began to remember the transpositions and didn't have to work them out each time.

Later he added a refinement.

'We need to have a security check, when you write. So I know the message really comes from you.'

'Who else would it come from?'

'What you do is you have some other secret sign embedded in the message.' (If I did not understand 'embedded' I wasn't going to ask.) 'Preferably something nobody else would notice. It should be something very simple, and something that's very easy to remember. Like putting the date the wrong way round, like Americans do, with the month before the day. Or put in the year but put it wrong. Put 1692 instead of 1962. They'd think it was only a mistake, see?'

'In this book I read there's this man, Richard Hannay. He breaks a spy ring. He knows how to be a spy. You should read it too. Anyway, he learnt from hunting in Africa, from watching the deer he was hunting, seeing how they freeze on the spot and merge with their surroundings. Perfect camouflage. So even when you know they're out there, you can't see them. That's what spies do. They merge, blend, try to be like everyone else. To be indistinguishable from their surroundings.'

'It's not like that here. It's not like your story. It's just ordinary here. Everybody's ordinary.'

'That's it, silly, that's just the point.'

He said that we should write everything down. If we wrote it all down a pattern might emerge.

'Write what?'

'Start with the evidence. All the things in the house that we know were hers.'

'That's hardly anything.'

There were the clothes that I'd tried on with Susan, the jewellery box – or not the box, that came from Dad's mother, but the things in it, the good things that he'd given her and the cheap things that she'd bought, and a few other things like a rosary that came from one of Dad's aunts who was very holy, and a funny little black cat that she brought all the way from Germany. I knew about the cat. Peter didn't. It was made of fur and wire, with pale bead eyes and a frayed ribbon about its neck. I told Peter she brought it from Germany in her pocket.

'How do you know?'

'She told me so.'

'It's got a name on its collar. Sophie Schwarz.'

'That must be its name then.'

'Suppose it must be.'

Peter didn't like me knowing more about it than he did.

'So what do we do now?'

'The next thing is to write down what we can remember. I've got exercise books for us. I got them from school. We write down who she saw, what she did. How often she went out, and where, everything. You put down what you remember, and I'll do mine, and then we'll compare what we've written. That's what you do. It's important to do it separately, without talking about it first. If we talk about it we influence each other's memory, make the other one think they saw things they didn't actually see.'

He got the books down from his room.

'And don't think too hard first. Just go and start doing it and see what happens. Memory's strange. Some of it comes from the unconscious. You've got to let it come.'

He was too serious, insistent. It scared me.

'You know it wasn't true, what you said about her being undercover. You know you were only saying it.'

He took my wrist and held it in a wrist burn.

'Then what's it matter if you write this? You won't be doing anyone any harm.'

So I took the exercise book back to my room and wrote. I put it beneath my clothes in a drawer. Every now and then I took it out and added something else as it came to me. I thought there was going to be a whole book but I covered only a few pages. You'd think there was so much to say about a person but when they're gone the record doesn't amount to much. It diminishes them. She took us to school, she had her hair done, she went shopping. (I was recording what she did. What she was didn't come into it.) Margaret came in the morning, she had a cup of coffee with Margaret, Margaret went. On Tuesday or Wednesday or Thursday, the butcher's van came by, or the grocer's, or the laundry. Peter thought it especially important that we record things like that, the regular things, in case one was a contact. He said there would have been some regular contact, a way of passing material or messages.

'It couldn't be the butcher,' he said.

'Why not?'

'Remember once he ran over a dog on the road? Mrs Jones's dog, that little terrier she had? He ran it over and it was dead. I saw. And he went to her and owned up. A spy wouldn't have drawn attention to himself like that.'

The laundry came and went in a grey box with a leather strap around it. It would have been easy to put messages in, folded into the sheets or inserted between the lists on the pages in the laundry book. The laundry man had a funny twisted leg, as if it had been ironed in a crease. I told Peter he was wounded in the war.

'How do you know?'

'Mummy said so.'

'How did she know?'

The next day he came we greeted his van on the road and talked to him as he got down from it and limped to the house. 'Have you two got somebody looking after you now?' he asked, and Peter was quick and said yes, there was someone in the house all of the time, though it wasn't true just then, it was the afternoon and Margaret had gone and there was nobody else there. I knew he did it to make us safe, just in case, but it made me afraid of what might happen. When I went to bed that night in the clean laundered sheets I felt the coolness of them and smelled the starch, and they seemed too white. I could sense their whiteness even with my eyes closed, as if there was a bright light that would not let me sleep.

Besides the tradesmen there was hardly anyone. It had not seemed to us before that this was odd and yet now we saw it. There was nobody from the past: no family, no relations, no old friends who came to visit. There wouldn't be, would there, said Peter, seeing where she came from? But there were no friends from the present either, from the time since we were born. She almost never had anyone come to the house. She went out. Sometimes she used to dress up and go out, to Cheltenham, Oxford, London even.

Maybe she saw friends then. Who these friends might have been we couldn't begin to guess.

'How about Mrs Lacey?' I asked. 'She was her friend.'

'Mrs Lacey couldn't keep anything a secret.'

'Mr Lacey then?'

'He was with the Japs too. He's just as cracked as she is, but inside so it doesn't show. He looks almost all right, like a proper colonel, an old soldier, but he isn't, he's fake. They wouldn't use someone like that.'

Of course we couldn't tell Susan. Sometimes I thought Peter liked that. He knew that all this spy stuff put the two of us apart from Susan and tied us to each other.

Peter was brilliant with facts and systems but he couldn't deal with stories. He should have seen that making up stories was easy. If he'd done it more he would have understood that. You made up a story and then you could turn to it when you needed it, and sometimes it might be true and sometimes not but that wasn't what mattered the most. What was difficult was telling your story to somebody else. If you did that it got stronger and more real, and then you didn't have control any more.

I tried to give the blue exercise book back to him.

'I'm not doing this any more. We haven't found anything. We're not going to find anything. There's no point. It's only a game.'

I said that to hurt him. I knew it wasn't a game.

'You can't do that,' he said. 'Not now. You can't.'

'Yes I can.' I threw it down at his feet on the kitchen floor.

Peter may have been small and thin for a boy his age but he was much stronger than I was. He grabbed me, and took my arm and bent it up my back so it hurt like it would break, and forced me down over the table. There were glasses and knives and things on the table, hard, sharp things close to my eyes. I saw the edges of them shiny and glinting, too close to focus, and shouted at him to stop, and his grip was so hard I didn't know if he would.

'All right,' I breathed, and again, 'Stop,' and, 'It's hurting,' and, 'I'll help you,' and there was a pause when he only held me and did not press any more, and then, slowly like a machine winding down, he unclenched and let me go.

It was raining, a heavy summer rain that made every-thing that was green go soft with a weight of water, leaves weeping from the trees, stems from the borders hanging over the lawn, plants splayed with the wet. It was a rain that fell straight and did not touch the window, so that you could stand with your nose to the pane of glass and see clear through, see it falling in fine lines that showed up where the trees were dark behind. A day like that was quiet and strange after so many days out in the sun.

Susan phoned and I said I couldn't see her, I was finishing a book and I'd see her later.

'Bookworm,' she said, but didn't seem to mind.

When the rain stopped for a time a pigeon flew low across the lawn, slow as if the air was too wet for flying in. The pigeon's feathers were the same heavy grey as the sky. I didn't want to go out, or see anyone at all. I sat at the table in the kitchen waiting for Margaret to leave. Margaret did the washing up with heaps of suds and didn't rinse them off so that they bearded the plates that she put on the rack. My mother used to tell her to rinse them but she was a stubborn sort of girl who you couldn't expect to change. She stood there at the sink like the cows in the milking parlour at the farm. I wrote in my book that the yellow Marigold gloves she wore went on to her big pink fingers like milking teats.

'What's that you're writing?' Margaret turned and suds dripped on to the floor from the plate she was holding.

'My diary. It's secret.'

'You two and your secrets. It's no good for you to be alone all day.'

'I think it's fine.'

'When I was your age there was five of us kids about, and the house not half the size of yours.'

'We like it how it is.' I didn't see that Margaret had much ground to stand on. Everybody knew that Margaret's youngest sister was having a baby even though she wasn't married. Susan said that at least Joyce had had a boyfriend. Joyce was pretty. Margaret was plain and her acne would put any man off kissing her.

When the washing up was done Margaret took the gloves off and draped them over the taps.

'Are you still there then? What are you waiting for?'

'Nothing. I'm just sitting. Writing my diary.'

'Well, you'll have to be off now out of here as I'm cleaning the floor.'

'But you did it yesterday.'

'And I'll do it again long as it keeps raining and it's muddy outside and you two traipse in and out without so much as wiping your feet let alone changing your shoes.

That's what I mean, there's nobody here telling you what you should and shouldn't do.'

And she pushed the sponge-headed mop right up to my feet, and I lifted them up so that it could pass beneath.

'Come on, you know I need to go under the chair as well.'

I took up the diary and locked it, and walked out where the floor was still dry.

Peter was in the sitting room.

'Has she gone?'

'Not yet.'

'I wish she'd get a move on.'

He had a screwdriver.

'What's the screwdriver for?'

He hid it behind a cushion when Margaret came in at last and said she was going, and we both went to the door and watched her leave, putting on her raincoat and leaving her footprints in a pale track across the wet lino.

'Here, you've got to help.'

The radiogram ran across half the length of the wall behind the sofa. It was a piece of furniture almost like a sideboard, of some yellowish lacquered wood veneer and angularly modern, a block on tapered brass-tipped legs; ugly, which was why it lived behind the sofa, but our parents had chosen it not for its looks but for the quality of its sound. To move it out we had to move everything else first: the sofa itself, the chairs to make space for the sofa;

then take the lamp from it, the books and records, the ashtray, lay them out on the carpet just how they'd been so that we could put them back right.

'What are you going to do?'

Peter began to unscrew the back panel. He took each screw and laid it neatly in the ashtray.

'But it's still plugged in.' I pulled the plug from its socket.

'It wasn't on, silly. I won't get electrocuted if it's not on.'

He had all the screws out now, laid the back panel on the floor. There was more space inside than I had thought. There wasn't much there really, just the speakers, one on each side, and a kind of board with knobs and wires of different colours and blobs of silver solder. He poked around like he knew what he was doing, only of course he didn't.

'The Krogers used a radiogram. They had it connected to a transmitter, and to an aerial in the roof. They had direct radio communication with Moscow. Their radiogram was just an ordinary one, like ours, like anybody's, but it had a high frequency band so that it could get reception from anywhere in the world, and it was fitted for headphones, so they could listen just with headphones, and these were hidden in the back of it.'

'Well, there's nothing hidden in this one.'

'The Krogers did the communications for the spy ring, see. Lonsdale was liaison. He ran the spies, did the recruiting and made the contacts, fixed the rendezvous and the dead-letter drops and everything, and the Krogers did the communication with Russia. They made messages and documents into microdots and stuck them into the books that they sent abroad. They were second-hand book dealers, that was their cover. They sent books to Holland and Switzerland and places, places no one would suspect and where someone else would send them on to Moscow, and books came the same way back to them. Even when Lonsdale wrote letters home to his wife they went that way, in microdots. Most weekends he used to go and see them, like he was their friend, and he'd take them everything he'd got in the week and Helen Kroger made it into microdots. That was what they found in her bag when they arrested her, microdots, and when they magnified them they found out that they were letters to Lonsdale from his wife in Russia, and one that he had written back to her.'

I tried to picture my mother with these people.

I saw her in her big winter coat, a lipsticked smile in the fog. The fog made the background wash away like in a poster for a film. I don't know if it was the first time the thought had come to me, or if it had been there for days or weeks.

'If she was one of them, then she was a traitor.'

'No. She couldn't have been a traitor,' he said.

'Why not? How do you know?'

'She wasn't English. You can't be a traitor if you're not English.'

Oh. Just that.

'Like Gordon Lonsdale, he was a Russian. He was a spy, but he wasn't a traitor. So people didn't mind about Lonsdale. Some of them even rather admired him. His letters were read out in court and everybody heard how he had a family in Russia and he hadn't seen them for ages, like seven anniversaries or something, and his daughter was having a bad time at school, and his wife wanted him to buy her a dress, only he couldn't exactly send it as a microdot, could he, and he seemed like a normal sort of person, for a Russian, and a patriot. Like a soldier on the other side in a war. You fight him but you think he's OK because it's his country he's fighting for. It was the others who were the traitors, Houghton and Gee. They just sold their country's secrets for money.'

'Did they get executed?'

'People don't get executed in England any more. They're going to abolish it.'

We moved the furniture back then and Peter plugged in the radiogram and switched it on. The radio made a little spit like it always did when you started it up but that was all. Not even a crackle.

'It just needs tuning.'

Peter turned the knob, pressed the buttons that changed the wavelength.

'You've broken it.'

Peter's face went very red as he went on working the switches and nothing came out.

'What have you done?'

'Let's play a record and check that.'

It was opera, the first thing that came to hand. The volume was turned right up. A woman screamed and made us jump.

'That works, anyhow.'

Peter lifted the needle and clicked it back. Then there was only the sound of the rain outside. I had a sense that there had been a time when it had lightened, a little earlier, when the rain must have ceased and the sun almost broken through and the room brightened. Now it was dull again, the room a negative space filled with the pointlessness of the afternoon.

'He won't find out for ages.' Peter spoke in a whisper that was like the rain. 'He'll never know it had anything to do with us.'

'But he'll find out sometime, won't he? And you won't be here, you'll be back at school. What am I going to say?'

'You don't have to say anything. Just don't admit it.'

Before he went back to school Peter said, 'There's someone we haven't thought of, I only just thought of her. And she's Jewish. Lots of Communist spies are Jewish, like the Krogers, and the Rosenbergs in America. Why didn't we think of her before?'

I hadn't mentioned Mrs Cahn because she was mine. I was the only one who knew her. I think even then I didn't want her touched.

'You're talking rot. You always talk rot. Anyway, Mummy never even went into her house.'

That wasn't quite true. My mother had gone in, the first time. I could remember her going into Mrs Cahn's front room and looking about it with approval. It wasn't English at all, that room. I think it felt like Germany. The piano was German, a Bechstein. My mother would have approved of that, would have put out a hand to stroke the polished wood. She was always touching things.

Every Tuesday she used to take me, in the car or on foot if it was nice. There were always a few words with Mrs Cahn at the door, standing on the step or maybe just inside the hall if it was raining. How they got on to the subject of the seaside that time I could not recall. Perhaps it was the one time she went in and she saw the photograph of the beach. Or perhaps it was a fine day with a high blue sky and one or other of the women voiced a memory or a longing.

'She didn't used to chat to her or anything. She just used to drop me off and go away.'

'Didn't they talk German?'

'I think they always spoke English. Probably because I was there.'

'What did they talk about?'

'Just about the weather and things.'

'What things?'

'How I was doing. What I had to do for practice. Nothing interesting.'

Peter looked critical, as if I had missed something.

'Really, Peter, that's all.'

'I should have been there. There must have been something.'

'It'd be just the same if you were there. If anyone was there. Just ordinary talk.'

'There are things like coded words, you know. Signals and things that spies use. You have to listen out for them though. You have to have an ear.'

*   *   *

'See who comes and goes from her house. See if there's anything odd, anything at all, anything that changes from one week to the next.'

'There won't be anything. Nothing happens there.'

She wasn't anything to do with Peter. I didn't want her to be a part of it.

Yet he was very serious. His thin face was tight with seriousness, his eyes fixed. I said that I would do it because he was just about to go back to school and I felt sorry for him. His knees looked funny beneath his big school shorts and his hair was newly cut and bared a white stripe on his neck where the summer sun hadn't reached.

'You will do it, Annie? And write to me if anything happens. You know how.'

We sat close together on the bottom step of the stairs. His trunk and tuck box blocked the hall but the door was open to outside where Dad had gone to bring the car up to the gate. Peter's hands were fists. The skin on them was stretched so tight you thought you might see through it, like a rubber band you pulled too far. I was glad that I did not have to go away yet to school. We sat and did not move as Dad took the trunk, though it was heavy for him, heaving it up between his arms and lumbering with it down the flagstone path. Then he came back for the tuck box and took that away.

I sat because Peter did, tight.

'I'm sorry, boy, we really must be going.'

He was panting a little from all the carrying. There was a particular look he had when he was out of breath, his face drawn out and mask-like.

'It's a fair old way and we don't want to be late.'

Peter's knees went close together so that I thought that he would not go, but he put out one hand to the banister, and then the other, and sort of pulled himself up. It was as if he was not eleven years old but a much smaller boy.

We went out in silence. Dad closed the boot of the car over the trunk. Peter got in the front because it was his journey. I would sit there on the way back. Usually it was dark when we came back from his school. We went in the daylight and came back in the dark so that I knew the way there much better, knew the roads and the turnings and the towns one way round and not the other. I sat in the back and pressed my face to the window, or sometimes wound the window right down and put my head outside so that the wind blew my hair along the side of the car, as separate from the two in the front as if there was a plate of glass between us, as if I was in a taxi or driven by a chauffeur. Like that I used to watch the trees and hedges pass, and sometimes I used to narrow my eyes and play a game in my head. I used to tell myself that it was indeed the hedges that were passing, the hedges and the road on the move like an endless tape being wound by, while the car itself and all of us inside it were perfectly still.

His school was down a long drive, a tall house of reddish brick with a turret on one side and long windows. We said goodbye in the hall, standing close to the entrance and with the length of the room stretching away. It was a long room and high like a church, with a dark wooden staircase at the end of it and a floor of polished tiles the colour of dried blood. Peter vanished in it quickly. He was lost among the other boys, all of them dressed and seeming to look the same, and the hard space echoed so with their running about and shouting that I was glad to leave.

2

My father is on his hunkers in the herbaceous border. It has rained in the night and the soil is soft, so that the weeds come up in his hands and he hardly needs to use his fork, but only pulls at them and then chucks them on to the path in loose green heaps to be raked up and put in the barrow later. I had taken the rake and helped for a short time but that was boring and he didn't seem to notice, so I put the rake down and only looked, and now there is nothing to do.

I start to pick some flowers to take into the house. There are almost as many flowers as in the early summer. There are roses still and other summer flowers in second bloom, and September flowers that have aged and heavy colours, like golden-rod and red and amber dahlias, and the tall purple monkshood behind them – and this I know that I must not pick because there is poison in it. Even if you only pick it, the poison could enter through the skin.

I look at the monkshood close, see the leaves that are glossy like health, the narrow cowled flowers, the shadow in them.

'Does a person die straight away?'

And my father smiles, and he says no, that isn't how it happens, only that they would be sick, or sleepy, and very ill perhaps if they actually ate the plant.

'You shouldn't grow it,' I said.

The piano teacher's house was at the other end of the village on a street that led out towards the main road. It was a plain street squeezed up against the hillside, the houses all much the same, stone houses with narrow windows right on the pavement that you could see into, china ornaments arranged on the sills for you to see, empty armchairs in neat front rooms. Sarah Cahn's was set back from the rest by just a few steps, so that there was space for the plants that grew up the walls and hung close about the windows that time of year.

Inside, the house felt quite apart from the rest of the village. I had always thought that it was like abroad. Now that I had been abroad I could say that, that it was like the Continent. The room where I had my lesson was the one at the front, where the sunlight fell in narrow streams in the late afternoon. There were lots of dark things in the room and they glowed: the shining wood of the piano, the paintings, the bowls of blue and red coloured glass that made spots of colour on the walls behind them. Sarah Cahn herself was a slim dark woman with a soft voice. There was a smile, a greeting, a question about how the holiday had gone.

'OK,' I say. The light on the piano keys makes them look cool, like water.

Daphne Lacey had driven me there in the car. She was going somewhere and she was late, as she always was, and we had left in a rush and now I was not ready to play. She had chattered all the way. Daphne Lacey was always turning her head as she drove and saying anything that came into it. I would have preferred her to keep her eyes straight and look at the road like my father did and speak in that impersonal, measured way in which proper drivers spoke as they drove. Or not spoken at all. Then there would have been time to separate the pieces of my brain, the music from all the words, Daphne Lacey's words, Peter's words before. Next time, I thought, I shall walk to my lessons, like we used to do, before. I shall walk alone; they'll let me do that now. I shall be a girl carrying a brown leather music case and the music will already be there in my head when I arrive, and nothing else. It will be close, and I shall sit straight down and play. If I do that, there will not be this horrid pause at the keyboard, this moment when I look down at my fingers and they seem stiff and separate, and frozen.

'Wait,' says Mrs Cahn.

Sarah Cahn has a soft voice, soft and composed. Peter does not know that. To Peter she is only a name.

'Wait,' she says. 'Don't start yet. Come and have a piece of cake first. As it's the first day and we have not seen each other all summer.'

Her clothes were dark like the things in the room but she wore a scarf with rich colours in it that glowed like the pieces of glass. No one else dressed like that in those days. No one wore black in the country. It was a smart, urban, Continental colour. People probably thought that Sarah Cahn was beautiful, but in an uneasy, unconventional way. Her eyes were dark pools. Her face and hands were always on the move but her eyes were still. Sometimes, when she played something on the piano and stopped, and I looked at her, I had the feeling that I might fall into them.

'I like your kitchen.'

A girl's voice coming out clear and poised as if she was acting, as a grown-up woman might speak when she visited another's house. As my mother might have spoken, as she had trained me also to act. With my mother there were always words to fill a space, smooth words that passed the required time with a shop assistant or a taxi driver or a piano teacher, and carried no meaning beyond them. Yet I meant what I said. I did like Sarah Cahn's kitchen; it was the nicest kitchen I knew. It was small, so that if someone sat at the table you could hardly get between it and the cooker, but it had a fireplace in it which was cosy, and the window looked straight at the green hill slanting up close behind.

'Has your brother gone back to school? You must be lonely when he goes.'

'So-so.'

Then no more words for a while but only cake.

Find out about her, Peter had said. Ask her things. Maybe they met some time when you weren't around.

She had her back turned, busying herself about the kitchen. Mrs Cahn was not like Margaret or Daphne Lacey. She understood that there were times to leave a person be, when a person did not want to speak. Almost, because of this, I felt that she was the one person to whom I might have spoken. And my mother might have spoken to her also, might have been friends with her even, and not just because of where they came from but because of the sort of people they were, because of something they shared, because they were both different from everybody else; but there had never been anything more than politeness. There had been only the coolness of my mother at the open door, and Mrs Cahn's eyes turning a little aside from her, or somehow looking down, looking to me.

On the mantelpiece was the photograph from the beach. You could hardly see that it was a beach really, just an old photograph of the little thin girl who was Sarah and a fluffy-haired woman who was her grand-mother, sitting side by side, big and small, in a funny kind of basketwork chair with a hood. The child looked as if she had been plonked down like a doll, her legs too short to reach the ground. There was no sea in the picture, just grey space behind where the sea must have been.

'You know the place you went on holiday, the seaside, the place in the picture? Did you ever see my mummy there?'

'Oh I shouldn't think so. Anyway I was so young when I was there, I wouldn't have known. That photo is from the last time we went. 1931. We couldn't go there after that.'

And then later I asked, 'Is it still there now, that place?'

'I imagine so.'

'Is it through the Iron Curtain?'

'Yes, it's behind the Iron Curtain.'

'And do people go there?'

'I'm sure they do, just like we always did.'

That wasn't what I meant. I meant English people, people like us, going behind the Iron Curtain. I asked if people could go through the Iron Curtain to live, if anyone defected because they wanted to live there instead of here. There was a famous dancer that summer who had defected from Russia. He was in Paris with the Russian ballet, touring, and instead of going home he had run away at the airport and asked if he could stay and dance in the West. I asked if it was possible for people to defect the other way.

'I imagine they could, only nobody does. Only spies who are afraid of getting caught. Nobody else would want to.'

*   *   *

In the room with the piano were other, newer photographs. There was a wedding photograph of Sarah Cahn and her dead husband. Mr Cahn looked happy but so thin that I thought that he must have been sick already. And there was one of Sarah, quite grown-up, with the people who she said were her second, English family.

This time when I sit down to play it is easy.

'See. That's lovely,' she says. 'Even when the mind thinks it has forgotten, the fingers remember.'

There were spies in Peter's mind, and others in mine. There was a book I had about Violette Szabo, who was a spy in the war. Peter hadn't read it. He thought it was a girl's book because it had a woman on the cover.

I had read the book that summer that was gone. I had read most of it in a day, lying on my tummy under a tree in the orchard, moving round when the sun got too hot or too bright on the page. I liked the book so I read it again. It told you how a woman might become a spy.

Violette was a London girl but French because her mother was, and she had a daughter but it was the war so she left her daughter behind and was parachuted into France to work with the Resistance. The first time she went to France she brought back a dress for herself from Paris, and another for her daughter that was too big because she could not tell how much her daughter would have grown while she was away. The second time she went, she didn't come back. She was ambushed by the Germans and captured in a gun battle and taken to a camp. Just before the end of the war they decided to execute her.

They took her and two other English women who were spies and lined them up and shot them.

Violette had violet-blue eyes, it said in the book. She was a tomboy and brave, braver than her brother. She showed that when she went to do her training, training with men and doing as well as them even though she was smaller. She trained to do soldier's things, to use a gun and fight with her hands and to operate a radio transmitter, but also she trained to be someone else because in France she was to have false papers and a false identity. Her name and everything she wore even would be different, everything French and nothing connecting her to who she really was.

I dreamed that, the strangeness of being someone else. I dreamed it for myself, and I dreamed it for my mother. When Violette was trained she had to learn her cover story down to the finest detail: the whole life history of the other person she was to become. She was drilled in it by her instructors so that she might convince even under interrogation. Again and again she must repeat to them where this other woman was born, the memories of her childhood and of every year of her life. I did this also. I made whole constructions of invented identities and drilled myself in them. I had all the details worked out: names, places, schools, friends, incidents, favourite colours, clothes, bicycles owned, things the person I was liked or didn't like to eat.

When I dreamed the story for my mother it was set not in France but somewhere cold beyond the Iron Curtain. It had to be there because that was where people disappeared. Sometimes she was working for one side, sometimes for the other; or she worked for both, first one and then the other, doubling layer upon layer until even I was unsure which one came beneath. But whichever the variation, the place did not change: a flat, dead land; bare earth like plough with a layer of mist upon it; tracks running into the distance; then a city that rose up suddenly out of the land, a flat cityscape with apartment blocks, all the same, one after the other, down long streets, and blank figures in a fog. There was no sound to the city, not many cars but no sound even to those that there were, and no colour.

I was staying the night at Susan's. If my father went out late I stayed there, or sometimes I did out of friendship, because we had decided that we could not be parted. A friend like Susan was easier than a brother.

Susan's room was very plain, quiet like Susan herself so that if she was not in it you would not have seen that it was hers. Her bed was in the middle of the room with a pink candlewick bedspread on it and a pyjama case in the shape of a cat, and because the room was big there was another bed just like it against the wall. On this bed a real cat slept, the Laceys' soft grey Persian. If I went into the room in the daytime I would often see it there, and it would uncurl itself and stalk away at the intrusion. When I stayed the night I would hope that it would return and curl up at my feet or on the blanket before my stomach. I used to wait for it, eyes open in the dark, listening for silent paws.

'Do you have daydreams, Susan?'

'Everybody has daydreams.'

'But, do you think you're someone different?'

'Sometimes I think I have other people in my family, lots of sisters doing things. I'd like to have lots of sisters. Four. Or maybe three so I'd be the fourth.'

'You don't ever want to be someone different yourself? Like a boy?'

'Why would I want to be a boy?'

'Because they can do things. People let boys do more than girls.'

Susan yawned.

'Do they?'

'I think so. Don't you think so?'

Susan didn't answer but it did not matter because I could hear the cat's claws snarl in the bedspread where it hung down to the floor, anticipate its weight about to drop on to the blanket.

'Do you ever think your parents might be someone else? Do you ever dream that?'

'I don't know. I'm sleepy.'

I stayed awake a long time. The cat was so close that I could not distinguish if its purr was sound or vibration. I would not move or turn to sleep until it was gone. Susan's breathing was steady in the other bed. What did it mean to be Susan Lacey? Quiet Susan, sleeping in the closed circle of her family. The Lacey history was known. It lay about the house in carved knick-knacks and ivory figures, pictures of tigers on the stairs, photographs of rubber trees and tiger hunters in the downstairs loo. The Laceys were rubber planters in Malaya. Daphne Lacey's family had been planters too. In the war, Godfrey and Daphne had had a terrible time when they were prisoners of the Japanese. Susan was a Lacey. She had red hair and white skin that burned as soon as she went in the sun. She had left Malaya when she was too small to remember it but she was a Lacey all the same. Planters transplanted, growing in England. My father said that there were lots of plants that liked to grow in England because it was a gentle place. They came wrapped in newspaper from the nursery and he planted them in their beds and told me where they came from, and it seemed that he named every country in the world. Sometimes they had soil of another colour sticking to their roots, red soil or peaty black soil. If the soil and the roots were dry, he would put them into a bucket of water overnight before he planted them. Peonies came from China and rhododendrons from the Himalayas. Laceys came from Malaya. Even if they lived almost next door and Mr Lacey drove every morning to work in an office like everyone else.

I asked Susan once if she planned to go to Malaya.
'Why?'
'To see what it's like.'

'But it's all changed. It's not the British Empire any more.'

Susan had no curiosity. Susan wasn't brave like Violette.

One weekend there was a snake in the garden. It was a brownish-greenish colour and stretched out on the stones of the wall at the bottom of the garden, where the lawn ended and there was a kind of ha-ha, the wall holding back the side of a ditch before the field. I thought at first that it was a stalk, a long and bendy stalk, but then I knew.

When I went towards it the bright sun threw my shadow ahead of me across the grass. Just as it was about to touch, the stalk moved, like a streak of oily liquid, and was gone between the stones.

I climbed down into the ha-ha and looked at all the gaps in the drystone wall.

'What are you doing?' asked Susan.

'I saw a snake. I'm looking where it went.'

I had an idea of what I was looking for: some round, perfect, snake-sized hole with edges polished by its body.

Susan stood well away from the edge of the ha-ha.

'Come back. Come up here. It's dangerous. If there's a snake I'll tell Daddy and he'll come and kill it. He knows how to kill snakes.'

'That's cobras. We don't have cobras here.'

'You're not supposed to be in the field anyway. You're trespassing.'

Some days later the snake was there again. This time it was my father who saw it. He said that it was a grass snake, not an adder, and that there was nothing to fear. You could recognise an adder by its markings, which were a kind of warning. The grass snake was basking, he said. Snakes didn't have warm blood like people and animals. If they wanted to be warm they had to come out and lie on warm stones in the sun.

Later he called me.

'Look!'

'Daddy, you caught it! I didn't know you could catch a snake.'

'Nor did I.'

He looked pleased as if he had won a race.

There was a huge glass jar we had, that sometimes my mother had put whole branches of flowers in, of lilac or blossom in the spring. He had caught the snake in a sack and put it into the jar, just so that we could see it.

It was trying to climb the sides and slipping down, again and again, as if it was writing lines of waves on the glass. The glass was clear and the underside of the snake was pale, whitish, pressing against it. I went so close I could see the golden rings about its eyes. But my father said that the most acute sense a snake had was touch, that it saw through vibration, that it could feel all along its body.

I thought how the glass would feel: so cool and smooth, even where there were bubbles buried inside it, and all of the length of one's body becoming the same cool temperature as the glass.

'I must let it go in a minute.'

'Can I just show it to Susan?'

'If you're quick.'

I ran to Susan's and called her.

'Ugh. I don't want to.'

'But it can't hurt you. It's in a jar. And grass snakes aren't poisonous anyway.'

So Susan came, and stood far back and didn't say a word.

I went right up to it and touched the jar where the snake was moving on the other side of the glass.

'See, it's fine.'

Peter wrote a letter every Sunday. It arrived the following Tuesday. The post came while I was at school. The envelope was always addressed to Alec Wyatt Esq., as no doubt he had been instructed, so I did not open it but put it on to the kitchen table so we could could read it together when my father got back.

We knew what it would say even before we read it. *Dear Daddy and Anna, How are you? I'm all right. The film last night was* Angels One Five. *It was quite good but I thought* The Dambusters *was better. We played a rugger match yesterday but lost it 23–7. Not so bad because it was the other school's first team and we're only the seconds. Only two weeks till half-term. Love, Peter*. That was his formula.

There were things you said that were always the same and it didn't matter what they meant. All that mattered was their presence on the page.

Sometimes I saw the letters that my father wrote back. Often they were two or three pages long, and his writing was small. Nothing formulaic to them, and that was to be expected. My father was so much better at writing things than at saying them. Sometimes he put drawings in his letters. This week there was one of the snake in the jar, and two figures of girls with enormous eyes running away. I thought that wasn't fair. Adults changed things to suit their purpose each time they told a story. I decided that I would write a letter of my own to say the truth. I wrote it in his code. *22 September 1692. Daddy caught a snake and put it in a jar. I touched it.* At least, I had touched the glass just where its body touched.

'I was playing something when you came. It's Schubert. Shall I play it to you? There's a lovely passage I've been working on.'

Sarah Cahn always carried a faint cloud of scent with her, carried it perhaps in the soft fabrics of her clothes as much as on her skin. I remember that. I remember how, when I sat on the piano stool beside her, I could sense her body like the snake, feel the length of her there, and yet I did not look but knew it unconsciously and saw only her hands, slender strong precise hands, that reached sometimes across my awkwardness and showed a fingering or how a phrase was played. And when the notes died there was the looking into her eyes again and a sensation of falling.

She plays the Schubert, seated beside me on the stool.

The score is held in a pool of light. The rest of the room has fallen into dimness. The wood of the piano glows, and the pages of the music are white, lit bright and so dense with notes that I cannot see where it is that she has begun to play.

'Turn the page for me.'

I catch the place in the music just in time, turn and hold the page, and look to see her eyes run on along the bars. Her cheeks are wet with tears.

Her eyes are wells with water moving in them.

I look away, out of the window where there is light still on the snow.

I thought of her this morning, in Charlottenburg. I was going to the museums there, walking rather indirectly from the station. There was a little public garden that drew me, with lawn and benches and big trees and azaleas, and apartments looking down on it. I continued down a wide street lined with tall limes. The apartment blocks there were substantial bourgeois buildings, five or six storeys high, many of them still with nineteenth-century façades, iron balconies and tall pedimented windows. Most of them you could not see into. The windows on the ground floor were generally shielded by hedges, those on upper floors high, blank behind curtains and blinds. Only when one was opened, its glass flashing in a rare moment of spring sunlight, was there a glimpse of what was within. It was no more than a notion really, of a high ceiling and a piano and a brown sideboard, and on the sideboard the gleam of china and glass that were like Sarah Cahn's. I thought how she must have sought out such things in England, some-how, in those years after the war, she and her husband deliberately composing or recomposing in the foreign place they had come to the home that they had lost.

I knew so little about her. She was only a passing figure, one of those adults who passed by in your childhood, who you knew so partially. Who you loved for a moment, who you might have loved more, if you had not been the child you were. Who you began to understand only years later, when you remembered them and saw the meaning in their actions, and saw just how much they might have mattered.

On one high balcony pots of tulips put up straight green shoots towards the sun. Sarah Cahn might have lived in such a flat. She was one of those people you could imagine in old age: deeply lined and white-haired but alert. If she lived up there, the sound of her playing would float out of the open window above the street.

Autumn 1962, the Cuban missile crisis. No child could have missed the sense of it. My father came home and watched the News.

The names of Kennedy and Khrushchev. The fear in grown-ups who perhaps expected war to happen because war was what had happened to them.

He poured himself a glass of sherry when the News was over. Occasionally he had a sherry instead of whisky, and ate with it a little piece of fruit cake. He would give me a piece of cake too, and a token sip of sherry in a small glass. When Peter was away I became his privileged companion. In the days when it was still light outside we would walk at this time about the garden. He would say, 'What did you learn at school today?' or, 'Are you being nice to poor Mrs Lacey?' as if looking after me were hardship, and I would have some little story to tell him; and he would smoke a cigarette and when it was finished press its butt down into the soil so that it did not show. But it was autumn now. In the garden it had long been dark, and even the Michaelmas daisies were finished. When I came home from school I got wet brushing by them on the path, the long stems that had fallen under a weight of October rain. I could see what he felt, sitting there, how the length of the dark evening seemed to stretch and sag before him.

He sipped his sherry and I saw the melancholy of the idle moment in his face. It was an adult moment with a preoccupation in it that a child could not break.

He put down his drink, picked the last crumbs of cake from his plate. He said that there was something special he wanted to hear on the radio, and I didn't know how to stop him. He went to the radiogram, switched on, tuned, turned the volume.

Nothing.

Again. Nothing.

'Have you listened to this lately?'

'No.'

It was true. It was not a lie. And that was all. He didn't mention it again. That was like him. He didn't see or he didn't tell you off, and you felt guilty about it and the guilt went deeper.

I went to practise at the piano. I think that it was a conscious act with a conscious purpose, to fill the silence. Piano practice filled the house with order, with a picture of family life. A child knows that instinctively, how to create a mood. I played my scales. First one hand, one octave; then two octaves; then both hands; arpeggios after; C major, A minor, and so on. Going up and going down steps. A minor in the melodic, and then the harmonic scale. I liked the strangeness of the harmonic scale. Sarah Cahn said that it had an oriental sound.

'How about your pieces?' my father asked. 'Didn't you start a new piece last week?'

There was a piece but I had not played it since I brought it home.

'I'm only doing scales today.'

'I don't think I've heard it yet. Won't you play it for me?'

'Scales are important. Mrs Cahn says so. Scales teach your fingers things.'

And leave your mind free.

The thing about scales was, they didn't trick you into feelings. They were known and they were there, and once you knew them you could play them automatically, like a machine, only faster or slower. And your mind could escape elsewhere. Like a weaving machine, your fingers the shuttle. (Or like the girls I'd seen on television, girls my age who worked making carpets in Persia. What did those girls think of, all day long?) Black keys and white keys, hands, the reflection of them moving on the shiny inner curve of the keyboard cover. Sometimes when I was playing I had the sense that I could see the girl on the piano stool, as if I was in the ceiling looking down from above: a girl with fair hair falling out of its ponytail, a white sock slipped down towards her ankle, her hands playing and reflected back.

Mrs Cahn told me that my scales were almost perfect. I need not spend so much time on them.

'That's all right,' I said. 'I like doing scales.'

'Shall I find you another piece, something that you really like?'

She had shelves and shelves of music books but the spines were so thin that it was hard to read their names. She had a light like a tall desk lamp that pointed at the shelves, and some wooden steps that she used to get at the top ones. There is a special way that music books have of ageing, something to do with the softness of their paper covers, a way they have of yellowing like parchment or gently flaking and crumbling away. There is a dustiness to them, like old flaking skin, that makes it so surprising when you take one down and play what is inside.

'Chopin. A dance. A waltz. That's one of his easiest ones, you could play that easily. Some of Chopin's very difficult.'

She played it through and there was water in it as well as dancing, clear fresh water bubbling up out of the dusty books.

'Then how about this?' She went to the shelves again, adjusted the lamp and the colours in her scarf flamed as she passed before it. She took out books of popular music, traditional songs, jazz, went back to the piano and played snatches of this and that.

I did not know how to tell her that I really didn't mind doing scales. There wasn't anything I wanted to play.

'Take this then.' A wafer-thin book from a bottom shelf; she had to kneel on the floor to find it. 'You're a dreamer. This is music for dreaming. Listen.'

'OK, I'll play that one.'

She shifted across and I took my place again beside her on the piano stool. We worked through the first few bars.

'You'll see as it goes along,' she said. 'You'll work it out. The left hand ties it together while the right hand dreams.'

'What language are the directions?'

'French. *Lent et grave*. That means slow and grave. But you don't need to pay too much attention to them. Sometimes the directions in these pieces are little jokes, absurdities.'

'What are absurdities?'

'The man who wrote this was a little man, a Frenchman, rather odd, with a beard and a bowler hat and an umbrella. Think of that and you'll understand.'

Sarah Cahn's hands reached across and played it again, all through. I watched the music.

Lent et grave. Like a procession, men and women in black all in a line; but someone came and danced between them, someone in colour. A yellow butterfly among the mourners.

Her kitchen was the kind of room that kept the rest of the world shut out, all but the piece of it you could see through the window: the steep rise of hill, a stone wall with a break in it, a big oak just a little off the centre of the view. There were no curtains on the window so that even in the dusk the field was there like a charcoal picture framed in the bare rectangle, a part of the room and not outside of it. There were other pictures on the walls, real pictures. No one else's kitchen had proper pictures on the walls. There was a small lively painting of a little house by the sea, and some drawings of men's faces that looked as if they been done quickly with long fast lines but that had probably taken far longer. I thought that one of the men in the drawings must have been Mr Cahn as he was like the man in the wedding photograph in the front room, only less stiff and more alive. He had a rather broad, lumpy face, not handsome at all. I guessed that Sarah Cahn must have got used to his being dead by now because the kitchen and all the rooms I'd seen in the little house seemed complete just as they were; no echoes in them, no empty spaces like at home.

It had become a habit, after the lesson, to go into the kitchen for cake. I suspected that the cakes were baked especially for me since there was always one fresh and uncut the day that I came. They were rich and luscious, the sort of cakes you ate with a fork. Sometimes they were a little richer than I liked but I ate them to be polite. Sarah Cahn had something about her that made me feel that I should be at my most polite. Perhaps it was as a courtesy to her foreignness, which was unmistakable even though there was hardly a trace of it in her voice. I felt a need somehow to charm this woman, or perhaps it was only that I sensed that it was in my power to charm her.

'You have a fire in the kitchen. Nobody else has a fire in their kitchen.'

A cosy, closed house. As if it was her shell, and she curled within it, like the walnuts that went on the cake.

It was there, sitting at the kitchen table after a lesson, that she told me how she had come to England. There was the coal fire in the grate, cake crumbs on the cloth. There was a direction in one of the Satie pieces, *du bout de la pensée*, which meant 'at the tip of one's thoughts', and often there were passages of time like that, with light words and the fire rustling. This day it happened that the thoughts were spoken.

'It was because we were Jewish. A British charity said that it would take the Jewish children and find them homes to live in.'

I wrote about it later in my diary. No one I had known before had told me a story about their life that was a proper story, like a story in a book.

Sarah Cahn said goodbye to her mother in the waiting room of a railway station. It was in Berlin, a great station that I imagined like Paddington where the train came in when we went up to London. I pictured Paddington, the high arched roof, the great clock where we were told to stand if we ever got lost, pictured the platforms filled with a grey throng of children without their mothers, brothers and sisters leading each other hand in hand, and a waiting room like a great cave full of mothers weeping.

She did not tell all that, only about the waiting room. That the authorities had said that they must make their partings there, to keep things in order. That there was to be no display of emotion on the public platform.

She was just a bit older than I was. She had on a new dress, and had new clothes in a little brown leather suitcase, in two sizes as she would grow, and her bathing costume because England was an island and she hoped to live near to the sea – that she said lightly, with a flick of the hand. There was a number hung around her neck. The same number was on her suitcase and on her rucksack. In the rucksack she had the things she had packed for herself and some that her mother and father had given her to take. One of them was that photograph on the dresser, the photo of her with her grandmother on the beach. Not the frame. The Nazis would not have let her take a silver frame. They had not let her take her stamp collection either. They said that it was too valuable.

At one moment Sarah Cahn stopped to take a handkerchief from her sleeve and put it to her eye. I was astonished to think that an adult might cry about when she was a child. About what had happened twenty-five years before. I thought that she had told me the story because of my own mother, because she was without a mother. But it wasn't the same at all. Her story was entirely different.

'We came to England across the sea, and it was grey and rainy. I didn't think I should ever come to like it!'

'Didn't it rain in Germany?'

'Yes, my dear, of course it did, but I was coming to a new place, a new life, and I didn't think you could start a new life in the rain.'

I saw it then like a film: the girl Sarah, standing with her suitcase on the ordered platform. Arriving in the rain, feeling the English rain on her cheeks as she walked down the gangplank on to the dock where the strangers stared. Starting to live somewhere else in some other language.

The first thing Sarah played on the piano when she got to England, when she was taken into a house by a family and found a piano there, was 'God Save the King'. Her father had taught it to her before she left. You will need this, he had said, in England.

'I think I should go home now.'

'Shall I walk with you tonight? Will you be all right, going in the dark?'

'I've done it lots of times before.'

She had got too close. I didn't want her too close.

As I went out of the door I said, 'Next week, I want a different piece to play, one like everyone else plays.'

When I got home I wrote the story down. I wrote it in a letter to Peter as well. I told him everything Sarah Cahn had said, only I did not mention the tears. I put the letter in my satchel with my homework and next morning I posted it on the way to school. I hesitated at the last minute but posted it anyway. It was tricky, watching people. Once someone had been under suspicion, whatever you said or didn't say about them could become a kind of betrayal.

'I found Königsberg, I found out, it's in Russia. It's got another name now, that's why we couldn't find it before. It was all ruined in the war. The Russians captured it and everyone left, every single German. I found it in the encyclopedia in the library at school. They moved all the borders around after the war and bits of some countries became others. Königsberg became a bit of Russia. So there's only Russians living there now, and they speak Russian and all the streets have new names in Russian. They write Russian with another script so you couldn't read them even if you tried. I'm going to learn Russian when I'm older. Maybe in my next school. I'm good at languages, like Dad, particularly difficult ones. I came top in Latin last term. If I learn Russian it might come in useful.'

Peter home, his trunk standing on its side, a brown trunk with wooden ribs about it, big enough for a child to hide inside. Peter back with ideas pent up in him, all the thinking of the term. I didn't go into his room much those days even when he was home. It had become a private place, for him alone; or partly it may have been only that he had been away so long at school that the room had stopped feeling lived in, just sporadically used. His trunk or his weekend case was always in the corner, as if it was a hotel and he was ready to go, and there were dirty socks on the floor. There was a photo of our mother in a leather frame on his chest of drawers. It was a studio shot of her looking like a film star, posing with her head a little to one side, smiling, white teeth and light in her eyes and a sheen on her hair. The image of our mother but not as we knew her. I had another shot from the same series but was not certain if either was like her at all. The picture with the best likeness was the one Peter kept on the table beside his bed and took away to school with him. It showed our parents together just after they were married, somewhere in Berlin. They were wearing overcoats and hats because it was December, and there was snow on the ground. Our mother had her head up, cocked a little back, caught in a laugh that was so typical of her that you could almost hear it. In one gloved hand she held a white bouquet that was the only thing that showed it was a wedding, and her other hand rested on her new husband's arm. Our father also looked like himself in the picture, smiling only with the corners of his lips, standing just behind her and tall and solemn like a guard.

Peter had out on the table the model he was going to make, that Dad had bought him for the start of the holiday. It was a tank this time, a Sherman. Peter said that the best tank in the war was actually a Russian one and the Sherman was American and not nearly so good. He had laid out all of the pieces meticulously on the newspaper that covered the table, with the glue and the pots of model paint beside them, and the transfers that he would put on when it was all done, a number and a white star, held together with a clip so that he would not lose them.

'Was that the same kind of tank that Mummy drew for you?'

'No. I wanted a Panzer. I asked her for a German tank.'

The drawing of the tank had been a great event. Our mother never did pictures. Our father drew, but she didn't. Yet for some reason Peter had insisted that she was the person who drew the tank for him. He cannot have been more than seven as it was long before he went away to school. He made her promise to do the picture one night before he would go to sleep. And she must have sat up for hours, because in the morning she had put it out beside his bed: a lovely clean pencil drawing of a tank with all its details perfect, lightly shaded, all lightly done with a touch that was quite different from our father's more haphazard style of drawing so that we knew that it was really hers.

'Have you got that picture still?'

He had it in a drawer with two pieces of paper folded about it so that it wouldn't come to harm. On top were the letters he had from her, I could tell by the writing, and the long scrolls of his school photographs. It was an honour to be allowed to see into the drawer. I had not been so close to Peter for ages.

'It's super,' I said.

'Do you think, Anna, really do you think –' It was because we were suddenly so close that Peter began to confide, but in such a rush that he got caught up in his words and stumbled over them. 'You don't think, do you, that – you know, about the Krogers and all that, whatever it is, well –'

'What?'

When he got all tight like that the tears always came up to his eyes. He did not like people to see him cry.

'It was just something I thought. I just thought it.'

'What, Peter?'

And suddenly he grinned, as if it was a joke. As if it wasn't serious.

'Maybe she's there. Maybe she's in Russia. Maybe they called her back.'

And I laughed too, suddenly, when he said it.

'Look at the history, the dates. Königsberg captured by the Russians, April 1945. She turned up in Berlin early in 1947, in the British zone, and met Dad. What happened in between?'

'I don't know. I suppose they just never told us.'

'She was in Russia, that's what. The Russians took and trained her, don't you see? She turned up in the British zone, not the Soviet one. How do you think she got there?'

Peter had read about it all, worked it out. The Russians were clever. Even at the end of the war against Hitler they were planning for the next one. They were training agents and placing them all through the Allies' countries. They were using the time to get everything in place. It was all worked out down to the details. They put in a complete system of cells, even then. Some would be active from the start, with informants and spies on the ground. Others might be 'sleeping', all in place with covers established but waiting to be activated by a message from Moscow. There were sleepers all over the place. Like the Krogers when they first came to England. They just went around like that was who they really were, and set up their business, and everybody believed it. But there were others who came and set up their cover, and went on being sleepers for years and years, and nobody ever woke them up. Maybe the call just never came, or the contact was caught, or died, or knew they were being watched, and then the sleeper was out on their own. Then they might just stay as they were, being somebody else, or they might go, quietly, cancel their identity and disappear.

'How do you know that?'

'It's obvious they would, isn't it?' He had it all so sure, so pat in his brain he did not like to be stopped.

The Krogers, before they were the Krogers, when they were still in America and still the Cohens, had been part of the Rosenberg spy ring. Known associates, according to the FBI. And suddenly in 1950, when the FBI were closing in on the ring, they had disappeared. Their money went from their bank accounts and their savings were cashed but they left behind most of their things, jewellery, clothes.

'Maybe they were in too much of a hurry?'

'Maybe they didn't want them. You wouldn't want your old clothes if you were running away to be somebody else, would you? Not if you were in disguise and didn't want to be traced.'

I t was dark outside. Susan was round at the house one day after tea and Peter had the idea of going out.

'Let's go up the hill.'

'You can't,' Susan said. 'It'll be too dark to see.'

'It's not that dark yet. And anyway, the moon's coming up. It's nearly a full moon, I saw yesterday.'

'Your father's coming home. He'll wonder where you are.'

'He'll just think we're at your house, like your mother'll think you're here.'

'I don't want to.'

'Look, Anna's coming.'

We put on coats, balaclavas, gloves, all dark things as Peter said that we should not be seen. Susan borrowed Peter's school duffel as her own coat was too light. We took a torch with us, the only one we had. Peter said that as Susan was scared of the dark she could carry it. We went out and across the road, down the track by the farm.

The air seemed ready to freeze. There was a first star bright in the sky but no moon yet.

'It's dark,' said Susan. 'It's going to be too dark.'

'It's fine. Just follow Anna and hold the torch straight.'

The cows were in the barn, lowing, snuffling. The warm smell of the cows bedded on straw spilled through the slits in the stone walls. But once we got over the gate into the field everything was cold and silent.

'Where do we go now?'

'Up. We're climbing the hill, aren't we?'

The hill loomed round and black. The sky behind it was still some few shades lighter, and the ruts in the track where the ground was bare showed pale and clear in the torchlight.

'I think I want to go home. Will you come home with me, Anna?'

'You can't now,' Peter told her. 'There's only one torch.' He stopped and waited for her to get to him. 'Anyhow, you're not holding it properly. The light's wobbling all over the place so we can't see the holes in the track. Give it to me and I'll take it instead.'

'No, I'll keep it. I'll hold it straight.'

Then Susan was quiet for a bit and the torch was steady, and the three of us walked close together, but silently so that the others seemed hardly there. I felt my footsteps soft on the ground. The night stretched all around and nothing seemed to begin or end. My exhaled breath made vapour in the cold air and I imagined that all of myself could be vapour, dissolving out into the night. The village was behind, below. I saw the houses like closed boxes, squares of light escaping them.

'What's that?' said Susan.

'It's only an owl.'

'I'm scared of owls.'

'You're scared of everything.'

I tried to cut them out of my hearing. I would like to have been alone, all by myself in the night.

'Please, can we go home now?'

There was another gate, a stone wall. Beyond the gate you walked straight up the grass to get to the top of the hill. The track turned away and followed the wall, going round to the other end of the village where Mrs Cahn's house was.

'Come on, Peter, let's go this way,' I said, aware of them both again, remembering to be kind. (A last breath of the night held inside, like the breath before a dive.) 'Let's not go up the hill. Susan doesn't want to.'

'We said we'd go up the hill. That's what you said you'd do.'

'But if we go this way it's just as long a walk. Only it's down by the village and we can see the lights so we can't be lost. And we can go along the backs of the houses and see in, see what everyone's doing.'

So it was my idea. That bit of it started with me, not Peter. I hadn't meant this walk to have anything to do with the spy game.

It was easy walking now, the track skirting the hill and falling slowly back to the level of the village. The houses, the few street lamps on the road, the church tower standing against the sky. A scattering of stars beginning to show. Susan was happier now, even beginning to find the adventure in it, in the walk, the dark and the cold.

Most of the windows had their curtains drawn already but in the vicarage we saw the outline of a woman before the window just pulling them across.

'Do you think she could see us, Peter, if she looked up here?'

The curtains joined. The Vicar's wife was gone.

In some houses there wasn't a light in the room that gave on to the hill, but lights in corridors and other rooms behind, filtering through so that the windows had a grey glimmer like that of the television screen before the picture came on. We saw pieces of people passing inside but none that we could recognise, not until we came before Mrs Cahn's.

'Look,' said Peter. 'It's your piano woman.'

She was wearing a wine-coloured dress and a dark apron, the rich colour moving across the rectangle of the cottage window, going to the cooker and putting something in a pan.

'She's got someone with her,' said Peter. 'See, there are two places at the table, and wine glasses. I bet it's a man.'

As he spoke the man came in. He was tall so that we could not see his head properly, looking down at such a steep angle through the window. He was thin, dark-haired when he came into view. Peter was sure that he was foreign and I thought that he was right though I could not have said why. The man went up behind Sarah Cahn where she stirred what was in the pan on the cooker and put his hand under her apron and pulled her back towards him.

'Cooo,' said Peter.

I felt myself blushing in the dark.

He put his hand right across her and bent his head to kiss the side of her neck and then her mouth, so that all we could see was the wine-coloured dress and the darkness of his hair.

'We shouldn't watch. It's private.' For once Susan was right and we should have let her lead us. 'Let's go.'

'Not yet,' said Peter. 'I want to see his face properly first, so I know him.' And he went down the slope towards the window, running quickly, sidelong so that he did not fall.

He did not understand that the view was better where we stood, because of the angle of the slope. The man put his hand up the skirt of her dress and felt there, and her body fell back away from his towards the table that was laid. Then he knelt down before her and put his head between her stockinged legs and dropped the skirt down over it.

Susan and I moved together, turning at the same moment, walking on down the track, saying nothing.

Peter got to us at the gate.

'He went,' he said. 'Where did he go?'

Only then did we begin to snigger.

'What is it? What did you see?'

And the giggles burst and we ran home. It hurt to laugh and run at the same time.

The Laceys' dining room was big and still like a lake: a smooth mahogany table reflecting the light, tall windows at the end of the room, lawn and bare trees beyond and a cool sky.

'Mrs Cahn has a lover.'

Words like that rippled out to the walls. You could see that it thrilled Susan to say them.

It was a formal room that they used for dinner parties and then I imagine it would have come alive. I only ever ate there a few times, Sunday lunches, sitting stilted with a linen napkin on my lap that slipped to the floor, listening to adult talk and watching the candles burning down. This was one of the rare occasions that the room was used for anything else. Daphne Lacey had moved the candlesticks and the silver to the sideboard, and spread the table with envelopes and sheets of stamps and letters for the Women's Institute. The table was handy for projects like that: mailings and Christmas cards, and curtain making, fabric then spread across instead of papers, green baize laid beneath the electric Singer so that it did not scratch.

We girls had been dragged in to help and sat side by side with piles of letters and envelopes before us, Daphne Lacey at the head with an index box writing out the addresses.

'Susan my dear, what are you saying?'

'There was a man there, at Mrs Cahn's.'

'Well, I should think the poor woman could do with someone.'

She wrote with a fountain pen in royal-blue ink, the writing large and curly. It was the sort of writing I thought was never true, the expansive female script of invitations – 'Do come!' – and Christmas cards that were addressed to 'All the family' where the writer couldn't remember the children's names.

'We saw. We thought he was foreign.'

'There's no need to gossip about it.'

'You always do.'

Daphne Lacey put down the envelope she had in her hand and looked sharply at her daughter. Susan looked back, oddly bold. I saw them, mother and daughter eye to eye, Susan's flash of insolence reflected in her mother's flash of anger. I saw that Susan would end up looking like Daphne, would probably end up being like her. And then I thought: Since I had no mother no one could know how I would be. It was a free thought, like floating. I took up the top letter from my pile and put it into an envelope. The envelopes had a side opening. Mrs Lacey had been precise and told us that the correct way was to keep the opening to the right, the side she referred to as the window side. We sat with the windows to the right, long windows with deep sills, and on the sills two grinning china lions that looked more like the dogs they trained in the circus. Outside the window the light was silvery. The morning's fine rain had stopped falling and the sun had come through. Birds out in the winter sun on the Laceys' neat lawn, moving suddenly from one spot to another as if they were on springs.

Her voice ran on even when you didn't listen: high and clear and careless, forgetting that we were children.

'She hasn't had an easy time of it, Sarah Cahn. Why, they'd only been here a year when her husband died. I thought she'd go, back where she'd come from, poor woman, there wasn't anything to keep her here. They only came, you know, because he had a job at the school. But then I suppose there wasn't anywhere else for her to go. Not since the war.'

'She came to England before the war,' I said.

'Did she, dear?'

'She told me. She left all her family behind and came on a train.'

'Well, if she said so, then I suppose she did. Her husband came later anyway. He was in a concentration camp.'

'Was that like your camp?'

The question just came out. I knew as I spoke that it was a subject that I should not mention. Sitting there at that table drove conversation in a way that I could not control.

Daphne Lacey's pen held poised for an instant like a dart.

'It was a Nazi camp. It was German.' There was precision in her voice.

'German, not Japanese.'

As if the difference were no more than language.

Or climate: the Japanese camp humid in the jungle, men's shirts streaked with sweat, cicada noise and the calls of strange birds; the German camp cold, to my mind, always cold.

Daphne Lacey was writing again. More writing curling across the envelopes.

'It quite ruined his health, of course. He was lucky to survive but his health was ruined. He never looked a well man, not when he came here. I only met him once or twice but I used to see him about in the village. They had a dog, I don't know what happened to it, but they had a dog, a nice little dog, a spaniel I think it was. He used to walk it. You used to see him out walking. Not up the hill, I shouldn't think he could have managed that, but through the village. He had TB, I heard. Lots of them had TB poor things when they came out but then I suppose they had to count themselves lucky they got out at all.'

Why did they not explain things, those adults? They did not explain, they did not define, but clipped their speech wherever anything mattered; and we were left to fall through the gaps between their words. There was something about the Japanese, the hush of something appalling which our people had suffered, British men and women held in some slant-eyed oriental silence. Then there was the vast horror that concerned the Jews, deeper and more distant. (And there was what Peter had said about the soap. I had never forgotten about the soap. For a time, I had not felt easy washing any more.)

I have two days in Berlin and then I shall take the train to Poland. If there is time, I might go to see one of the death camps. All the tourists go there nowadays. Auschwitz is too far, but my guidebook tells me I might go to the smaller camp of Stutthof, which is close to where I will be.

Yet I do not think that I could bear it. Not now, not alone. Another time perhaps, if I ever come back. These are chill grey days, these days of German spring. Spring here comes later than at home though I understand the summer will be finer. Cold days reel slowly by and I let them pass. I see the sights. I walk the streets. I sit in cafés, anonymous. Thoughts become intense. It is because there is no one to break them. I observe, and I think my English thoughts. Those about me speak German and I see them from a distance as if they are no more than figures moving on a screen, subtitles lost, I the viewer, uncomprehending. I order another coffee. The present is less meaningful than the past.

'Stop daydreaming, dear. Come along, Susan's nearly finished hers.' Susan's pile of leaflets done, mine only half folded. Daphne Lacey's red fingernails on the pen, writing fast. The stamps still to do. There was always something still to do if you were Daphne Lacey. The mailing, the stamps, a drinks party, meals-on-wheels, some other thing.

As if being busy kept Daphne Lacey whole. As if all the pieces of her held together only so long as she was in motion. That if she stopped she might disconnect, fall apart, just cease to be.

He smoked some kind of cigarettes that had a heavy, dark smell, different from what I was used to – French cigarettes, I suppose they must have been, or Camels. I knew he was there as soon as I went in. I did not see him but I smelled the cigarettes, and saw his brown overcoat hanging on a hook in the passage between the entrance and the stairs. The door to the kitchen was closed. I imagined him sitting in the kitchen smoking, reading the newspaper, his chair pushed back beside the fire.

I was glad that I did not see him because I would not have known how to speak to him. With Mrs Cahn it was not so hard. I could play my scales, say the same things I always did, and forget about the wine-coloured dress. Today she was wearing a plain black dress that she had often worn before. She looked elegant, tautly poised as she always was, the same as ever. People did not change because you knew something else about them. They still looked the same. Only, if you thought of it, the way you saw them changed. There was the person you saw, who was always the same, and then there was the other person that you found out they were inside. Like Russian dolls. Or spies. Like Helen Kroger and Leontina Cohen.

Once during the lesson I heard him cough. (The tall man throwing his cigarette into the fire and sitting back, folding the newspaper.) The lesson seemed to go very fast, and I did not stay on for cake.

I was already outside, gloves on in the cold, when Sarah Cahn called me back.

'Wait, Anna. I had a little Christmas present for you, just a tiny thing. I had it all ready for you and then I forgot. Don't stand outside though, come in just a moment and I'll find it.'

She opened a door on to a bright strip of kitchen. I saw the sink, a wooden drying rack on the wall above the draining board, some cups waiting to be washed, the back of a chair. The man's coat was close in the passage so that I could smell the smoke on it, deep in the wool like its own smell.

'You can open it now if you like.'

'No, that's all right, I'll take it home and put it under the tree.' I said that even though we didn't have the tree yet. I just didn't want to stay any longer.

I didn't go further than the doorway because he made the kitchen crowded. You could see he was tall even though he was sitting, his legs stretched so far across the floor.

*   *   *

142

I had seen enough of the man to know him when I saw him again a few days later.

As Peter said, Christmas shopping in Oxford was only Mrs L's idea of fun: lunch at a Kardomah, and a visit to Father Christmas that we were too old for, only Peter said that we had never done it and Daphne Lacey had insisted, as if we were not just motherless but deprived. So we had to queue in the department store for what seemed hours, hot in our coats because Mrs Lacey told us to keep them on or we might lose them, all to see a cardboard grotto and a man with old teeth and a too-red face. Peter dragged behind all day, and Mrs Lacey kept calling him on crossly, looking hectic, her face askew so that you could not imagine that it was really any fun for her either.

We were in another shop buying a dress for Susan. Peter was hanging about the door waiting for us to leave. Just outside there was a three-foot-high plaster panda that had a green tray in its paws that tilted when you dropped money on to it so that the money went into a collection box. He had put in a penny, and a threepenny bit, and now he was experimenting with folded sweet wrappers and whatever was in his pockets.

'You shouldn't do that,' I said. 'It's for charity.'

'So what?' said Peter, and took a piece of chewing gum from his mouth and wrapped that.

Out on the street it was dark now. It had got dark while we were in the department store, and now that the lights were on the town looked happier than it had before, the lights bright in shop fronts and over the heads of the crowds that spilled out from the pavement on to the road. There was such a mass of people, you did not at first distinguish them as individuals.

'Look, it's him, the man who was at Mrs Cahn's. I saw his coat. There!'

It must have been the same one. It was a distinctive coat, unusual for England – for the country anyway, as I would not have known whether or not men wore coats like that in London – a soft smooth wool, expensive-looking, not so much brown as the colour of caramel. (Even when I had seen it in the passage I had thought: I will know that coat if I see it again.) And the man who wore it was taller than everybody around him. Even at that distance, fleetingly in the street, I knew that it was him.

Peter ran out.

'What are you doing?'

'Tailing him.'

'But you can't. We have to stay here.'

'This is our only chance.'

Peter was fixed, walking fast, cutting a determined line through the crowd, taking advantage of his slightness to nip into the spaces between people, almost running. I kept up as well as I could. I was already out of the shop and did not want to get separated from Peter too.

'Wait for me.'

'Don't you see, we have to get close or we'll lose him. There's such a crowd, we'd lose him in it.'

The man wasn't shopping. He was going somewhere. He treated the crowd like dust to be brushed through.

We would have lost him if he had not stopped. We thought we had lost him when we came to a slightly more open space and saw him cross the road to stand at a bus stop.

'Don't let him see us.'

'He doesn't know us.'

'He might do, sometime in the future. He mustn't know we saw him here.'

We stood beneath an awning on our side of the road. One bus came, then another, but the man did not get on either of them. It was cold, standing there. A third bus came and, just as it did, a woman walked up to the bus stop beside the man. I did not see where she had come from. I hadn't noticed her anywhere on the street till then.

A big, bell-like coat in a coarse dark tweed. That coat also I had seen before. From where I stood I could see only the back of it, and the back of the woman's head and the headscarf she had on, but I could have told you that on the front of the coat were five big tweed-covered buttons and two pockets set at a slant above the hips.

My mother's coat. I knew it immediately.

Peter saw it too.

Was that how tall my mother was? I couldn't have said. I suddenly wasn't sure that I could quite remember. But that was like the way she moved: that brisk, graceful way the woman lifted herself on to the bus, with the tall man standing aside and getting on behind her.

There were lights on in the bus but the windows were steamed up from all the people on it. We could just make out these two new passengers as they walked down and found seats. The woman first, the shadowy form of her settling in a seat that was spare beside a window, and her dark-gloved hand going to the window and with a waving motion beginning to wipe away a patch of steam, just as the bus began to move off.

We watched it go, the yellow clouded windows and the hand waving.

Peter went on watching as other traffic followed it away: a car, a van, more cars, a lorry then that hid the last of it from view. Another bus drew up at the stop. This one was almost empty. The windows were clear because there weren't so many people breathing inside. It pulled away, following the first one.

I was really cold now.

'Come on. We've got to find Mrs Lacey.'

I could not put words to what I thought I had seen. Looking about, at the street and the people, I could not so much as think which way we had come. The people's faces seemed all the same, the faces of strangers and nothing else, nothing more personal or individual, nothing in them that meant that they could be stopped and asked the way. And the street, I knew the street at least. That was itself, the shops one side of it, the long wall of some college building on the other, a gateway that had a tower like a crown above it – only I could not say if we had come up it or down.

'Where do we go? Where is it?'

I was standing in the middle of the pavement, looking along it, looking at the shop signs, not seeing what was close. I was in the way, jolted by one person and then another, jolted against Peter.

I grabbed on to him, his arm in its thick duffel, held tight as if I would be swept away if I did not do so.

Such a long time it seemed to take to walk back the length of the way we had come. A flood of people washing by, breaking before us; Peter walking on, turning every now and then as if to check that I was myself. His face was cold and strange. His hair was sticking up. I noticed that he did not have his hat.

'Where's your hat, Peter?'

'I dunno. I lost it somewhere. Maybe in the department store.'

At least he knew where he was going. He got us back. Daphne Lacey was standing in the street, holding Susan tight to her and quivering with anger. She walked ahead of us holding Susan's hand all the way to the car.

When we got home Dad was already back from work. The hall was full of the scent of the bare Christmas tree that he had just brought in and propped up against the stairs. I ran into his arms. I could smell the forest on him, dark and green and soft underfoot.

Building a card house brings the mind to a fine point. Concentration complete, brain to fingertips. Tongue to lips. Control.

The card is crisp and clean between my fingers. I am standing a nine of diamonds against a four of clubs. I work on the floor. I know from experience that the rug before the fireplace makes the easiest surface, its fine pile helping to support the cards. The only problem is if someone else were to enter the room and the vibration of their steps move along the planks beneath.

There are lots of packs but most of them are incomplete. We keep them for card houses. Dad has just bought two new packs for teaching us to play canasta. They have pictures of sailing ships on them, one pack blue, one yellow. The stiff new ones are good for walls. I will start by using them. I will build a lower floor, with rooms that are roofed and between them open courtyards, running all the width of the pattern of the carpet; and then with what cards are left I will make an upper floor. The older cards, which have worn soft at the corners, I use for roof, so far as I can.

Building a card house like this takes hours. That is what it is meant to do: to take all the rest of the day, so that I need think of nothing else.

The door opens. I hold still, afraid that a draught might spill it all. But the door is opened slowly, only halfway, and Peter leans on it, gripping it with his two hands.

'What are you doing?'

'You can see.'

Peter sags against the door as if he must need it to hold him up.

'Don't stand there with the door open. Close it or there'll be a draught.'

And he comes in, slowly, sits across the arm of a chair.

'The fire needs stoking,' he says. He is used to stoking the fire since there is no one else in the house in the afternoons.

'Well, you can't do it now. You can't get to it without knocking down the cards.'

'That's silly. It'll burn down.'

I take up one of the old packs, begin to lay a section of roof, dropping each card lightly from just a whisker's space above the structure, precisely across the joins and the walls.

'It'll go out and then we'll be cold.'

The fire is almost all red, most of the coal in it, which Margaret had put in earlier, either burnt away or alight. Just a few lumps at the tip remain black, like the peaks of a mountain range.

'Are you just going to do that, make a card house?'

'Yup.'

'All day?'

'Yup.'

I shall go on doing it until I have used up all the cards. Until it gets dark, until children's hour television starts, until we can go to the Laceys' for tea. Until Daddy gets home. Until there is something else going on.

Peter throws something across the card house into the fire. It is a dirty jelly baby that he must have had in his pocket for days. The little figure shows up for a moment against the red coals and then burns away.

'If you were a sleeper, how long do you think it would take before you forgot who you really were?'

'I don't know what you're talking about.' I am starting on the second storey. The first pair of cards slip on the shiny surfaces of those beneath and fall flat, but the structure holds.

'If you were living undercover for years and years. Wouldn't you get confused?'

'I'd always know who I was. I couldn't be anyone else.'

'How can you tell? You've never even been away on your own.'

'I just don't think I would.'

'If you didn't have your name. If you weren't Anna any more. If you didn't have any of your things, anyone at all who knew you from before. Not Dad, not me, not anyone. What then?'

'I'd still be me, wouldn't I?'

'Yeah, but who would that be? Think. You're speaking another language. You've got another name. Everybody

150

calls you by that other name. You've got friends, maybe even another family. Which person would be you?'

'I don't know, Peter. I don't know what you're going on about.'

Peter is not slumped any more but stiff, leaning forward on the arm of the chair. He is bent forward at an angle like his penknife when it is half-folded. Even when I concentrate on the card house I can feel him there, stiff like a knife above me.

'What if you've got a husband, children? What are they then? Just part of your cover?'

There is an intense moment of silence then he puts his feet to the floor and stands up.

'Don't stamp,' I say. 'It'll fall down.'

3

Margaret said the man's name was Istvan Kiss. Susan thought that was funny and did not understand why we two did not laugh as well. And he was a musician. The neighbours heard him playing the violin. That was noted in the village, that the widow and her exotic visitor played music together in the afternoons.

'Must be a Russian,' Peter said.

'Well, he couldn't be English, could he, with a name like that? Neighbours say he doesn't talk at all. Might not even speak English for all we know.'

'What language do you think they use to talk to each other?'

Of course the name was Hungarian. It wasn't a Russian name even. I know that now. He was only a Hungarian violinist. And yet there were nights when he loomed up in my dreams, following me through a crowd as we had once followed him, but the following never ended and I got nowhere against the flood of people, and he never drew closer and nobody stopped.

It was Peter I might have feared. Peter drove us into it. He made us think what we should not have thought. Peter made everything so complicated, his denial distorting everything around us.

Country children should understand about death: that it happens and it is there and that is that. Don't they see dead things all their lives? Myxy rabbits. Squashed hedgehogs on the road with their innards spilling out, tangled lengths of intestine in lurid waxy shades of red and blue. Dead birds that you can pick up by their feet or by a stiff wing and bury. In that winter that followed, that cold winter, there were many dead birds. Once I buried a thrush in a shoebox. I had found the bird close by the house, on the open snow. Perhaps it starved, my father said. Look how all the ground where it might have found worms is covered deep in snow, how the berries are gone from the whitened bushes. Or perhaps it had just died of cold. That was what I thought, taking it inside, laying it in the box on a bed of green tissue, noting when I brought it into the warm how soft the speckled feathers were on its breast. Of course the ground was too hard for digging. My father suggested we make a place at the bottom of the compost heap, the rough heap he had by the gate to the orchard. He lifted out chunks of frozen debris with jabs of his fork and made a hole where I laid the box, where there was brown soil beneath.

It was the winter of 1962–3, the great winter of my childhood, when the snow came in December and lay

156

right through until March. Thousands of English birds died that winter, garden birds and songbirds that were caught by the freak of the climate. It was many years before their population would recover. Years before the time would fade from people's talk.

The snow came two days after Christmas. We were having a posh lunch at the Laceys' when the snow began to fall in big feathery flakes. We ran straight out as we were on to the lawn. The flakes fell waveringly and lay on our hair, and on the grass and on the hard leaves of the shrubs. It fell in a soft silence that made laughter tinkling and distant, made distant the banging on the window that was the grown-ups calling us in.

'Here, come back! Who told you you could get down? Come in and put on your coats at least!' And when that was done the grown-ups went back to their meal, looking like a picture of themselves sitting at the table through the long windows, with the snowflakes falling before them. There were candles on the table, in the silver candelabra that were wound with ivy, and glasses with wine in them, and crackers stacked in piles like logs.

It was one of those full moments that make a memory, when everything else falls away. People later classify childhoods as happy or unhappy. Best would be to tot up these moments when nothing else mattered. That was what childhood was for.

For weeks (or perhaps it was only days and memory has extended them) there was no school and Peter was home, and our father was home because he could not drive to work, and everything was strange and in abeyance. Each morning when I woke the window panes on the casements had frosted with the night's breath into patterns like coral, and I looked out through the white coral branches to the sea-floor whiteness of the fields.

We wore woolly tights beneath our trousers. I had a white knitted hat with coloured pompoms hanging from it. Susan had one the same as if we were sisters. We would go out with Peter and meet the village children on the hill, though usually we did not know these children or passed them only blankly because most of them were from the council houses beyond the playground. Peter and I had a proper toboggan made of wood, an old one that was seasoned and polished from use, but many of the others had only trays. We let some of them have a go on ours, and then for a time they seemed to accept us.

There was one boy who was big with thick black hair, and he was the same age as Peter though he was much taller. One day he went with Peter right to the top of the hill, the two of them pulling the wooden toboggan together up the steepness of the slope. The toboggan came down like a bomb with the both of them on it, and ran on and on over the flattening field until it overturned in a drift where they had begun to clear the road. When Peter got up and shook the snow from him his face was as red and shiny as the other boy's, and almost I would not have known him for who he was at home.

The boy was called Richard. Richard to us though some of the others called him Dick. His father was cowman at the farm, and sometimes I had seen him with a switch in his hand making a man's coarse deep calls to the cattle as he helped his father herd them into the yard, the sounds coming strange and alien from deep in the back of a boy's throat. He was rough. He climbed our wall and took apples from our trees and I had seen him smoke a cigarette. It meant something to have him for a friend.

Once Richard led a gang of us round the hill past the back of Sarah Cahn's. We were looking for new slopes but this one was no good because of the wall that crossed it. The snow was very deep this side of the hill, a drift piled high against the trunk of the big oak there, more snow piled into its crotch and along its branches, even in the creases in its bark. The wall itself was almost hidden, only we knew where it was by the pattern of the drifts, and Peter, who had begun to show off a bit, clambered up and found the stones beneath and started to walk along it. Richard came up behind him, and another boy, though they went thigh-deep in the snow trying to get up. Susan and I left them be and pulled the toboggan along the track, even if the boys said we were sissy. It was smooth on the track and we got on ahead, putting our prints into clean snow, and heard the boys fooling around behind us.

The lights were on in her windows as we passed, but this time there was no one to see in the house.

'Mr Kiss is still there, if that's what you want to know,' said Susan. 'He's snowed up like everyone else. Mummy said that he's a professional musician and that there was a concert that he should have given but he couldn't get there.'

'Does your mother know him?'

'No, it's just what somebody else told her. Anyway, when you think about it the concert doesn't much matter because half of the audience wouldn't have been able to get there either.'

None of it mattered so much in this moment in the snow. It did not matter what we were doing. If the man was there or not there. If he was who he was said to be or someone else. Who anyone was. Who I was, or Susan or Richard or Peter. Peter was only a boy for now, rosy-cheeked, swaggering, loud unlike his usual self, leading other boys along the wall. 'There's a place I found,' he was saying, 'Further on. And there's nothing at the bottom of it, nothing to stop you. No road or anything. It just goes on and on.' Richard threw a snowball and then he was jumping off the wall into the deep snow and they were rolling over and fighting and running on with the snow on their faces and down their necks but too hot for the moment to notice.

Later, when the moment had passed, it all began to matter again. It came back to us just as the cold got to Peter later, when he was tired.

Peter was tired before Richard was, and Richard threw a snowball that smacked him in the eye, and in the shock of it Peter lost his temper and screwed up his face and his fists, and attacked Richard for real. Anyone could see what would happen, Peter so knotted and puny before the big boy, as if he was asking to be beaten, and he was beaten soon enough, crumpled and crying in the snow. His nose was bleeding; there was a thick dribble of blood running down, and he put a handkerchief to it but did not get up and only lay where he was, and for a moment none of the other children had the sympathy to go to him. We just watched for a moment as he lay in his temper and his cold and his pain and whimpered, and took the dirty handkerchief away to see how thick and bright the blood was, and put it back to his nose again; and then we all moved together, even Richard, and helped him home.

It was the same with the other thing. It had gone from my mind all of that afternoon and then as we walked home it came back suddenly like a shudder, as we dragged down to the road and to the village. Snow had begun to fall again. Richard and the other boy walked ahead, Peter behind but not so far behind that we could not hear him sniff now and then and feel his shame. Again we passed Sarah Cahn's, but by the front, with the car that must have belonged to Mr Kiss parked outside caked with snow. I did not look in. I knew how it was without looking, even though everything outside was changed and white. I felt his presence in the house there before we reached it, felt it in my spine falling back as we walked on.

Peter said the cold made it like Königsberg. Winters there were always like this.

The pond in the village had frozen up and some people cleared it of snow and went skating, but most of us didn't have skates and just slipped around in our boots and fell over. I'd never been on ice skates though I guessed it was like roller skating. It looked easy when other people did it.

Peter said that between Königsberg and the sea there was a great lagoon that froze beneath two foot of ice. When the city was under seige in that last winter of the war, the ice was the last way out.

'There had been big bombing raids in the summer, and the Russians had been attacking for ages, getting closer and closer. Everyone knew by then what was going to happen. For months, they'd been leaving, when there were still trains going and roads open back to proper Germany. They didn't believe Germany was so great any more, even if people in Berlin still thought so. They knew the Russians were winning. All that autumn, people had been going, and they went on going all through the winter. Even when the Russians had blown up the bridges and the railway lines and they couldn't get away by land any more, they got away by ship, but sometimes the ships were bombed by the British or torpedoed by the Russians. There was one ship that was torpedoed by a Russian sub, and sank with ten thousand people on it, all refugees, old people and women and children and babies, and they were all killed. Imagine that. And the Russians said it was a great victory and gave the submarine captain a medal. That was why the ice was such a good thing. It gave them another way out. They could walk out from the city over this great lagoon, safe between the land and the sea, where there weren't any tanks or any subs, and walk across, walk miles and miles in the snow and across the ice, and get all the way to Danzig, and that was still a German city. That was the way the last people got out. And the Russians finally captured Königsberg in April, and by then the ice was melted and there wasn't any way left.'

In 1945 our mother was sixteen. I made a picture for myself of a girl of sixteen walking miles and miles through the snow. When snow was like it was now outside, deep and soft with dark clouds hanging right down over it so that you almost thought you could touch them. When walking made you warm at first but after a while you weren't so warm any more and bits of you started to hurt with the cold.

I pictured the girl walking all alone but Peter said that there were thousands of people escaping all together. So I saw a great flock of people, dark on the snow, spread across it like a picture of caribou in the *National Geographic*, and the girl in the crowd but alone. She has lost her family somewhere. I knew that she had lost her family. Perhaps they had been killed in Königsberg before she left or perhaps she just lost them in the crowd.

Then, but it is quite some time afterwards, she turns up in Berlin. She speaks good English so she gets a job with the British and our father is working there too and that is how they meet. There is a story that will be told between them, told and repeated by their children when they have them: how she was working in the same office and noticed one day that he had a tear in his trousers and offered to mend it, and how she had mended everything for him ever after. The story used to be told like a joke, as if he only married her because she was neat and good at sewing, when it was obvious that she was pretty and lively and so much younger than him, obvious that there would have been competition and that there was some better reason for them to have chosen one another.

'Do you think that was the way Mummy went, across the ice?'

Perhaps she skated. I was sure that she would have known how to skate.

'How do I know? Maybe she did. Maybe she went before.' And there was the other possibility, that she didn't leave at all and was captured by the Russians instead.

*   *   *

I am practising the piano. My father is home and he likes to hear me practise. Never before has he spent so many days at home with us, and days indoors, snowbound, the garden where he might have spent his time even in the winter smoothed over so deep in snow you could not see a plant in it.

There is time to talk in these long days. I am going to ask him about Königsberg, about how all the people got out. That's history. He cannot mind telling me that. I'll choose my moment, find a good moment when he's ready to talk. Just now he sits in his chair with his eyes closed. It is impossible to tell if he is really listening. I have played the new piece without an error, note perfect, like an armour without chinks. If he has noticed, he does not show it.

I am about to speak but he speaks first. He has been listening after all.

'It's time we had the piano tuned.' There is a cigarette burning in his hand but he has not smoked it. Delicately he lifts it and tips the intact column of ash into the ashtray on the table. 'When did we last have the piano tuner here?'

'Ages ago,' I say. It has been two years, precisely.

'I'll call him straight away.' He gets up to find the number.

I'll have to ask him later, another time. I play the piece again. Mrs Cahn would want me to pay attention to tempo and dynamics now. Play it again, she would say. She would set the metronome. Listen, till you hear the pulse inside you.

'When will he come?'

'I don't know. I haven't called him yet.'

The idea sets off a tremor of possibility. The piano tuner came the day after it happened. They let him in and he spent some time alone in the house.

'Will it be soon?'

'I shouldn't think he's doing any calls at the moment because of the snow.'

There was no need for him to hurry, it was hardly an emergency, but he came the very first day that the road to the village was open, appeared at the door like a successful explorer flushed from the cold, with his little brown bag and stories of the depth of the snow at various points along the road. A man must work, he announced, and made a joke with a nervous laugh. A man could not just hibernate the winter through. Yet I thought that was just the sort of thing a man who looked like him should have done. He seemed even mousier now than the other times: a shabby brown man, his eyes exaggerated like those of some nocturnal creature behind the lenses of his glasses. He unravelled himself, shedding hat, scarf, coat in the hall, and under his great coat he had on a thick beige cardigan, and fingerless gloves that he kept on and that I thought somebody must have knitted for him, unless he had knitted them himself. There was something rounded and feminine to him that meant you could imagine him knitting.

It was like before. The tuning fork, the same systematic discordance, the same corrections, working down and then up the keyboard. The piano open, all its ribs and innards bared.

'How does it work?' I asked. 'How do you know when it's right?'

'I listen how the sound is made up,' he said. 'The whirring within the note, the frequency, the beats per second. Do you hear it?'

'Yes,' I said, but I didn't. I heard only jarring, tensions like lies, meanings withheld.

And he went on, insistent, precise, sound by sound jarring through me until I thought I could not listen any more, and then suddenly he was finished and he raised his hands, high wrists as if the fingerless gloves were gone and there were instead the black sleeves and white cuffs of the concert pianist, and played, at last, something fluent, fluid like Chopin.

'Lovely,' he said. 'A lovely little instrument. But you need a new string. You've a broken string on the low B. It's all right, there are two strings, it still plays, but I don't have one with me. I'll have to order you another one. I'll bring it round when it comes. Tell your mum that for me, will you? Tell Mrs Wyatt I'll be round with it, in a week or two.'

Two whole years gone by. How did he not know?

'You can tell Mr Wyatt,' I said. 'Mrs Wyatt's dead.'

His eyes seemed ever bigger behind the glasses. He fumbled with the tuning fork.

'Oh I'm so sorry, dear, I didn't know.'

'But it's ages ago now. Not last year but the one before. Just the day before you came.'

It was a kind of test: as if the sudden words might make his disguise drop off, all his shabby oddness, which might only have been a costume put on with his role. Only it didn't drop off, and he looked more embarrassed than ever, and put all his outdoor clothes back on and shambled out.

The piano tuner came that day, and the milkman and the post (the postman late, with so many days' worth of letters that they didn't fit through the door) and the delivery van from the shop. And when I went down to the shop with Susan that afternoon, I saw Mr Kiss go. Already we knew that there would be more snow coming. Even if you had not heard the forecast you could see it in the sky.

He was at the counter buying cigarettes, trying to buy his brand but they didn't have it so he had to buy some other – some plain English Virginia tobacco, but in a little village shop you cannot expect much choice. He looked hurried, annoyed, and brushed by us without seeming to see us; and soon as he had gone out he came back in to buy some matches, and bought them over our heads while we waited with Mrs Lacey's list. But when we went out with our basket he was just sitting there in his car. He had the engine running but he sat quite still before the steering wheel, smoking and staring straight ahead. It was just beginning to snow by then. The clouds that had lightened that morning and lifted away were weighing down again, hanging over the hills heavier and darker than the land. We had walked to the end of the road before the car drove off.

Such a pity he had gone, Daphne Lacey said. The blizzard had lasted all night and once more everything was clear and white, and the drifts had piled back across the roads and the village was closed off. Such a loss, when you thought about it. Why, if only he had not been in such a rush to leave, the snow would have kept him longer, and they could have had him give a performance in the Village Hall. That was what they used to do in Malaya, if anyone interesting ever came, they would put something on, at the Club, though the Village Hall was hardly the Club. And it was so cold besides. If only they could heat it properly. Those little heaters they had put in last year had scarcely any effect at all. Apparently the man was really quite a famous violinist. Surely that was proved by the way he had to dash off the moment the road was open. What a pity that Sarah Cahn had been so selfish with him. She could have shared him a little. There was nothing for her to be so cagey about. What an odd woman she was really, keeping herself to herself the way she did.

*   *   *

'He was lucky to get out,' Peter said to me later. 'It must have been a problem for him, for his contacts too. They have regular times to call in, you see, preset dates and times, and specific codes for each of them. If an agent misses one call he has to make the next, or they have some alternative plan, some fallback plan, with a special code to say if everything's OK. If he misses that one it starts to worry them. Moscow Centre wouldn't like it if he was snowed up here and disappeared from their radar altogether.'

'You don't really know that. You're just saying things.'

'At least I'm trying to work it out.'

'I don't see why you have to. Why you can't just leave things be.'

'Come off it, Anna. You saw. Like I did. Don't pretend you didn't see her.'

I had started to walk away and he grabbed at me. I was quick though and he only got my sleeve.

'Let go of me.'

'But you did see, didn't you?'

Everything was tight and going out of focus, like the moment before you cried.

'Let go. You'll stretch my jumper.'

And when he let go, I said, 'OK, I saw. But I only saw a coat. It could have been someone else. It could have been any woman. Lots of people have the same clothes, don't they?'

Peter sulked back to his room then and I took the

171

toboggan and went over to Susan's again, and we went out on our own to the big slope at the end of the village.

No one there but ourselves. And the snow new again, powdery over the polished crust of the slope. Even Susan is brave, without the boys to see. On the toboggan we are flying, gripping on to each other, hair whipping each other's faces, flying over the white ground.

Hold on. Hold on tight.

*M*arie, Marie, hold on tight. Words come back. Something about a girl on a sled, and her cousin the arch-duke. The opening of 'The Waste Land', just a piece of a poem that we studied at school. When I get home I will look it out. It must be there somewhere on the shelves, but such a slim book slipped in among all the others that I have not seen it for years. I have noticed this before, that when you are out of England things come to haunt you, words, books, pieces of knowledge that were taken for granted at home. Memories. Once I spent a whole holiday with my husband trying to remember the name of some film we had seen, something quite unimportant that it had occurred to one or other of us to mention – and this when we were young, before we had grown old and conscious of forgetting things. We were in Spain, travelling, inland where it was dry and wild and the plains stretched for hours before us. If we had met another person from England we would have asked, but there was no one to meet, only villages that were emptied with people hiding from the heat. Soon as we got home the name came back to us and we knew how very little it had mattered.

I do not understand the references in the poem. If someone ever explained them to me, then this too I have forgotten. Who the people are who drink coffee in the Hofgarten. (And where is the Hofgarten? Not Berlin, I think it is somewhere other than Berlin.) Who is the girl on the sled? I will need to have someone explain all this. All I understand for sure, understand deep down as you should understand a poem, is the piece about the spring and the lilacs. April is the cruellest month. It is April now and in Berlin it is still cold.

When my father died I went to his house alone and sorted out his things. Just me, no Peter. We spoke about it after the funeral. He'd flown back from Hong Kong. I hadn't seen him for a couple of years and he looked good, tanned and fitter than you would have expected for his age. Composed, slick even, every inch the successful lawyer. When he looked at me I knew he thought that I looked old. He offered to come to the house but I told him not to bother. No point his wasting time with all that, away from his family, away from his work. Anything he wanted, I said I would send. Partly I had done this out of consider-ateness and partly for myself, for distance, to keep the habit we had formed that kept the past at bay.

'You're sure?'

'I'm sure.'

Do what you want with the stuff, he had said. Take what you want and sell the rest. There would be nothing worth shipping all the way to Hong Kong.

'Don't you want to keep anything? Not even for your family, your girls?' There was a Chinese wife I'd met a couple of times when she made trips to London, two daughters I knew only from a photograph he once sent of them playing on a beach. I supposed that they had grown now and weren't little girls any more but I didn't have any other way to picture them.

'I think your girls should have something. I'd like them to. I'll look something out and send it.'

'Fine,' he said, and the word had no meaning.

The house felt strange, as if everything had been subtly moved. It should not have been so. I knew the place well enough. It had scarcely altered since we were children, and I had always been around, coming and going, particularly in the last months of his illness. Perhaps it was just that a house always feels different after someone has died.

I began by going through the kitchen, a bit of practical housekeeping, throwing out what few pieces of food there were that would rot, putting into a box what I might take home and use myself. I even cleaned a little. I felt a temptation to clean it all, cupboards and shelves and corners, all the things that an old man's eyes would have become inured to, but satisfied myself with the work surface and the sink, and made a note to myself to call

175

up the woman who occasionally came to clean for him and book her for a whole day to work through the entire house. I wanted that done before it was sold.

The simple work was activity at least, an assertion of the present in the stillness of the house. I put the kettle on, laid out on the clean worktop the makings for a cup of coffee, black coffee it would have to be since there was no milk. I walked through the rest of the rooms where the dust had settled, and felt that I was walking outside of time and outside of myself. Recent events, my father's illness and death, and distant childhood ones, earliest memories, seemed all of a piece, and from all of them I was detached, as if they were only dust and you could trail a finger through and wipe strips of them away.

It was with that sense of distance that I took the mug of coffee to his desk. I placed the mug with care on a loose paper though the leather was already ringed and marked and worn like old skin. I knew its surface well, the touch of the leather and the round wooden handles of the drawers, knew how I expected to find it, and yet it was different from that. It had all been rearranged. The papers of fifty years, which I had expected to find in their usual light chaos, had all been sorted and sifted and stacked.

This was the first moment that I had felt moved since coming into the house. So this was what he had done when he was ill, preparing things for me in his mild, considerate way. I felt him sitting in the same chair in which I was sitting now, methodically sorting drawer after drawer, muttering and filling a wastebin and the floor about it with all that could be crumpled and discarded. I thought of all those times I had rung him to ask how he was and what he was doing with his day, and he had said that he was busy. He didn't tell me what with, but now I saw. He had organised himself at the last. He had put out will, birth certificate, whatever it was you needed to register a death. Other things he had arranged in specific drawers: letters, some sketchbooks he had had in the war, odd photographs that had not found their way into albums, receipts for whatever in the house was valuable, keys to clocks, a compass and a cigarette case. There was a sense of emptiness in these drawers, of too much space there where they had been crammed for years with so many things that had now been dispensed with, tidied or edited away before they might again be seen. Even the smell of the drawers when they were opened, before I touched them, the smell of papers and dust and bared wood, suggested recent disturbance.

Many of these contents had been familiar all my life. I had looked in the desk before, officially and unofficially. Peter and I had gone through it, guiltily, in the days of our suspicion. Most of what I remembered was there. There was a game we used to play at children's parties, where we were shown a lot of objects on a tray and then shown the tray again, and had to remember what had been on it before and what had been taken away. I used to be good at that. I looked at the tray hard and tried to keep the image of it like a photograph, memorised it and fixed it tight behind closed lids, and opened them only when the next tray was put before us so that I could see in a flash how it was changed. Now I had the same feeling, only I could not have named any precise object which had been taken away. The odd thing was what had appeared which had not been there before, not when we had searched for it or any other time I had nosed through: our mother's diary. It was a blue Letts' pocket diary for 1960, with reminders and appointments neatly marked in blue ink, filled up right through into the few pages at the end that ran into the beginning of the January of the following year, right up to what appeared to be a doctor's appointment in Oxford the day she died.

I found it in the lowest drawer, the last drawer I came to. I put it on the desk top and riffled through the other contents of the drawer, and finding nothing more of interest closed it, closed all of the drawers in the desk before I read, careful and deliberate, starting from the beginning, page by page.

What Peter once would have given to see that. What I would have given. And now it had only pathos: the banality of it, of dentist's and doctor's appointments and beginnings and ends of term, the impersonal reduction of a life into a book hardly bigger than a cigarette packet. There was only one line written there that was personal in any way. That line. At the back, in the spare pages for notes, a phrase that I recognised at once: *lilacs out of the dead land*.

What would he have made of that, if he had known? If he had been there, if he had come with me. If he was not even then on his flight home, flying away back to being whoever he had made himself.

Look, Anna, see that!

A boy, holding me there by the force of his feeling – not the man who had become a stranger but the boy I knew too well, picking through drawers and files and papers. Thin energy. Quick fingers. Burning eyes. See that. See the tidied desk, the evidence of the house. See. I was right, wasn't I? I was right all along. No random event but only conspiracy. Some other hand, always, some hand other than our own, our mother's, our father's, dealing things out.

Even now, so long after, they had not forgotten. They had remembered, and come and searched and cleared and arranged. Determined what we would find and what we would not find. Made all this, the order and the empty space, a deliberate thing, arranged, composed, something more than the work of an old man tidying up for death.

So there. Told you so. The thought came to me and there was no holding it back.

I took the diary away with me that first day, and a cardboard box of food, nothing else. I loaded the box into the car and then went back and locked the door and felt the house behind it as it used to be, as if the rooms inside were still alive as they had been, and there was the smell of aeroplane glue in them and the coal fire burning.

You have to remember these things, Anna. Don't write them down. You can't write them down anywhere but you've got to remember them always.

As if we were followed, watched, liable at any time to interrogation. And I was a child and confused and could not get them straight, the codes and checks and fallbacks, systems of communication and operation, all that trade-craft he tried to teach me, that I understood only in fragments. How even the connections are concealed, how each agent is isolated, never knowing more than is necessary for them to know. How a single phrase, some quite innocuous phrase or a line from a published book, might identify them or hold the key to a cipher.

I drove back home and did not have the strength to get the box out of the car. I would get it in the morning and sort everything then, tins of tomatoes, stale coffee, outdated herbs, half-used bags of sugar and flour that would hang about and sadden the larder for months. I only took the diary in.

My husband and daughter were in the kitchen.

'What's that?' my husband asked.

A slim blue book, a frayed blue ribbon hanging from it. An object of such familiarity that I did not really need to say.

'You OK?'

'Tired. I'm just tired.'

He opened a bottle of wine, scrambled some eggs for our supper. I put the diary away in a drawer.

Soon afterwards I happened to see there was an old film about Violette Szabo on television. I had nothing better to do that day so I drew the curtains and sat down and watched it in the afternoon. The film was made in 1958 but I had not seen it before. I had read the book when I was a child but I had not seen the film.

There was a recognition code Violette used when she met a member of the Resistance.

Violette: It's good that spring is here at last.
French garage mechanic: It was a long winter.
Violette: And now the days are drawing out.

Virginia McKenna did not look like the Violette I had imagined.

I would have to put the pieces together, I saw then. For myself, if the past was ever to make sense. Go back over the stories, the stories I carried in my mind and the stories that were real. Visit the places where they happened. When there was time, I would go and find out for myself whatever was to be found.

When my daughter came back from school she was surprised to see the curtains drawn. You've been watching telly, Mum. Then you can't stop me from watching now.

There was something I had to see, I said. Something that reminded me of when I was a child.

It was so very long, that winter, longer than any other winter that I have known. The winter of the Great Blizzard. In the first weeks it was an event: pictures on television of Gurkhas breaking through to the snowbound, helicopters making air drops, factory workers sent home, farmers pouring away milk that could not be collected in warm white streams across frozen white yards. And then the snow did not go. Temperatures did not rise. The cold, the snow, the shovelling happened every day. And when milk was delivered it froze on the doorstep if you did not bring it in. The cream froze up through the top of the bottle and pushed off the silver lid.

A hard winter. Hardest of all on Sarah Cahn. I would not have known the term depression. I think people did not use it so much then. I made my explanation from the one piece of her life I had seen, and that piece only, which was the affair and the man's leaving, and some melodrama about it. I might see it differently now, knowing the history, having some idea of her experience. What I knew then with certainty, with a child's sure empathy, was that for her the winter was longer than for anyone, alone again with the snow outside and the village cut off sometimes for days on end, living through it day after day, weeks going by, and each day as still and lonely as the one before, and the loneliness intense because the man who had been there was gone.

When my father was home he liked to walk with me to my lesson. We had to walk some of the way along the road where the pavement was piled up, walked in the tracks of the few cars that might have gone through the village that day. When we got to the house there might be no more than a single set of footprints before us on the path up to her door, going and returning in a loop so that you knew that it was only the postman or the milkman making his delivery, or there might be none at all, those of previous days filled up, new falls of snow covering over where it had been cleared before. No sign of her going out at all.

One time she was playing the piano when we came so that she did not hear us, and we were kept out waiting in the cold.

'I didn't know,' my father said, 'that she could play so beautifully.'

'She came from a musical family, in Berlin. Her father was a conductor.'

'Your mother said that we were lucky to find her here.'

We had to wait until there was a pause – now and then she paused, went back, repeated a difficult or unsatisfactory phrase – then knock again, hard, and when she came to us at last she looked at us for a moment as if she did not know us, or as if she had come from very far away. I thought that that was how she must have looked when she first arrived, when she came off the ship and saw that everybody was a stranger speaking a strange language.

'I'm sorry,' she said. 'I'd forgotten the day.'

'I understand,' my father said, 'it's all a muddle since the snow.' He stood a moment and looked uncomfortable and then went away.

'You shouldn't knock so hard,' she said, after he had gone.

'There's no need. I am just here. You knocked so hard that I thought it must be someone else.'

At some point during that winter I noticed that she had begun to lock the door even when she was in the house. That was strange to me. People didn't do that in the village. At home you just walked in and out, and didn't lock the door even when you went shopping, and when you went to someone's house often you just walked in the back door and called. Yet at Sarah Cahn's now there was a delay, the sound of unbolting and a key turning, sounds of boxes and secrets. And once I came inside she went back and locked it again, and pushed a rolled blanket up to the bottom of it. She said that it was on account of the draughts, and that made sense of the roll of blanket but not of the locking. Locking the door didn't keep you warm.

Then it's not only that he's gone, I thought. She's frightened of him, that he might come back.

It was cold in the house, and dark. The only light that was on was the one at the piano. Even the passage that she had come down to the door was dark, and the fire had gone out. I began to play my scales as Sarah Cahn fetched kindling and coal and remade the fire, and then wrapped herself up in her coloured shawl and fed the fire as it began to burn.

'Shall I play my pieces now?'

'Why, yes. What are you playing? The Diabelli, wasn't it?'

'No, that was ages ago. I did that for my Grade Three.'

'Of course. You played it very nicely.'

She didn't remember, though. I could see that.

'You gave me something new to play. We started on it last week.'

She tried to recall herself but she was restless — or maybe it was only that she was still too cold — and came and stood behind me as I played, and did not sit as she usually did, so that I felt ill at ease and the notes sounded hard and uneven.

'Did we talk about the tempo? You have to be very precise here.'

She took the metronome and set it, stood it on the top of the piano.

There was the tock of the metronome, the sound of the fire, the metal stick of the metronome moving from side to side. I tried to concentrate, to loosen my fingers and play. Though I could not turn to see, I knew that she had wandered away again, across the room to look out on to the dark road. I played right through to the end of the piece. Usually she would stop me after a few bars or lines and correct me, and I had to go back over them. This time I did not believe that she was listening. I got to the end where the piece repeated, and started again at the beginning, and I knew but did not care that I had speeded up, that I should be stopped and held back.

Then there was chocolate, a warm mug in my hands, but the kitchen was cold.

'This weather, this winter, goes on and on. Even you children must be getting tired of it by now.'

'Oh but we like it. I think all winters should be like this.'

'Sometimes children go by on the hill. Do you go up there? I've wondered if you were one of them. When you're all wrapped up in coats and balaclavas I can't tell.'

'Sometimes.'

'We had much more snow than you do, when I was a child.' She spoke in a way that I remembered later as strange and sad – but perhaps that was only because of what happened later, perhaps I did not hear it so at the time but only a plain story about a city that had forests beside it, and lakes that froze and where they might skate if there had not been too much snow. Sarah Cahn said that she too had a toboggan, which she pulled along with a friend. Like you do, she said, when you go past on the hill.

*　　*　　*

My father's car outside. Sarah Cahn unbolts the door.

'Look, the snow's falling again. Like feathers, do you see?'

Where the light from the open door slants across them the big flakes do indeed seem like feathers, slow and swaying like feathers as they fall.

'Sometimes I think there'll be so much snow that we'll be covered over, all those feathers pressing down on us.' She speaks lightly, with a little fragile laugh.

I get into the car. I know precisely, with all my senses, what the words mean: the muffling weight of cold feathers, white and grey feathers piling up, lightness becoming weight, and not a comfort but a suffocation. Like when people are smothered with pillows. Sometimes people are killed like that. It is how people kill others that they love, the kindest way, how mothers kill children who are in pain and whom they cannot help, when the children are asleep and do not know. When Sarah Cahn speaks about the feathers, I feel that it is not a metaphor she is speaking, not an expression of what something looks like, but how it is, how she experiences it. When she says that about the snow I know that it is, indeed, suffocating to her.

'I don't want to do piano any more.'

I say the words before I have really thought them, and know as I say them that that is not precisely their meaning. It is not piano I want to finish with, not even Sarah Cahn either, not exactly. It is the things that the piano, and Sarah Cahn, make me feel.

'Why's that, poppet?'

'I just don't like it any more.'

'But you play so well. Everybody says how nicely you play.'

I do not feel safe in the car even though we are only in the village. The windscreen wipers groan, those big loose flakes of snow coming at the glass, stubborn ones holding to the blades and being pushed to and fro.

'Keep it up a bit longer, won't you, Anna? You know your mother loved to hear you play.'

'I don't want to.'

'She used to play rather well herself once. Before you were born. After that she never seemed to find the time.'

I persist, even though this information is new and at other moments I might have followed it up and the opening that it makes between us.

'You let Peter give up the clarinet.'

'That was only after he'd been away at school. You're going away in September. Let's talk about it at the end of the year, when you've seen how it is there.'

'But that's *ages* away.'

'It's not so long as all that.'

'Then let me go now. I want to go there now.'

The road before the headlights is like a tunnel, the tyre tracks that we must follow becoming whiter even as we drive into them.

'Look at the chords,' Sarah Cahn would say, 'and you can work out what key a piece is in. Look at the notes at the beginning, and then again at the end. Sometimes there's a note missing but you can work out what it is. You'll find it's all much easier then.'

Music theory made little more sense than Peter's codes. Only I saw that it was like his codes, which also depended on patterns and keys, which worked once the keys were deciphered, which related to one another this way and that and changed accordingly. Intervals and thirds and fifths, and the same notes in each key but they meant something different, and sometimes the one note was a sharp and sometimes it was a flat as it switched from one key to another.

They made it so complicated. I did not see why things must need to be so complicated, why they could not simply be what they appeared to be. Like the spy thing. I did not want to believe it or not to believe it. I just did not want to think about it. I did not want to see how all the people connected, if they connected, if there was a pattern or if there was no pattern at all. I was not always sure if this was what Peter wanted even. Sometimes when I saw him I thought that he really meant it, but Peter always looked as if he meant everything. Peter looked earnest and tight even when he thought he was joking, which was why things he did, even his teasing, could hurt so. I could not know if he really thought it all through at school when he was away, or if he only thought of it at moments when he was on the edge of things, when he was falling asleep or waking, or when he was coming home, travelling between the school-boy that he was and the other boy that he was at home. I did not know if it was real for him or just a game, a distraction.

Sometimes spy rings were organised with people called cut-outs, Peter said. There were agents in the field and there were spymasters who ran them and the agents and spymasters never met but there were people called cut-outs between them, who were go-betweens and nothing else. This meant that none of the agents knew anything but their own work and that, if one of them was captured and interrogated, the others were not threatened and the ring could not be broken.

One thing I wanted to ask him. What if you cut out the cut-out? If you did that, wouldn't the connection die? Then the agent at the end of it might be left alone, just himself or herself again, just as they appeared to be.

When Sarah Cahn rang to cancel a lesson, I was glad. I could go over to Susan's instead.

Mrs Lacey was cooking sausages for tea.

'You're early today,' she said. 'Did she let you out early?'

'Mrs Cahn's ill,' I said. 'She's got a bad cold.' She hadn't given any reason but there were lots of colds going round and it was quite possible that she had a cold.

'Oh, is that what it is? Oh I'm glad it's only that. I'd heard something about her. One of the women in the shop said that she'd come in and that she'd looked not at all well, and was rather odd, and went straight out again without saying a thing. I'd been thinking perhaps someone should go round and see her.'

'I'm sure she's fine,' I said, not wanting to be sent. Once or twice I had been sent with Susan on an errand of mercy around the village. 'Except that she has a cold, of course. She said she just didn't want to see anybody. Not till she's better.'

I drove by the house a couple of days later, driving somewhere with my father. The days were long now since it was March, but not bright, just dull and persistent like the snow. It was teatime when we passed and there were no lights on in the house yet I felt sure that she was there. It would have been just bright enough to see from inside, to see who was out on the road. As we went by I knew that Sarah Cahn was in there, no more than a density in the darkness, in there with the doors locked and the lights off, standing with that Indian shawl she had wrapped about her, seeing the car pass.

When the next week's lesson came round, I decided not to go. I had never done anything like that before. I took up my music case and pretended I was going there but went another way altogether. The village was grey and quiet and there was no one to see me.

It had been a bleak day with an iron sky but without wind, so that it was not so cold as it looked. The snow was soft and wet now, dirty everywhere it lay in the village. It was time that it was gone. We were used to it now, we had had our winter. Everything looked closed and forgotten. The smoke from chimneys merged too soon with the sky and even the lit windows looked barely alive. I walked past the playground and saw that the slide and the swings were bare now of snow, and went on the swing for a long time, back and forth, watching the roofs of the houses opposite coming towards me and going away; and then closed my eyes and saw the roofs again in my mind, coming and going.

Then I saw my mother watching the roofs, watching in that same evening, that same twilight, that same thaw, only the roofs were higher and blacker and massed together, the roofs of a city. Sometimes I saw my mother like that, shut away somewhere in a dingy room, far away, somewhere in the dead land in the East – Europe of course, not Asia, but a kind of Europe that was referred to only like that, as the

East. She was high up, in a room up flights of narrow stairs, and always looking out, standing at a window that was closed. The room varied a little each time I saw it, but it would have flaking paint or old scratched wallpapers (the colours of them drab, if colours could be seen) and the closed window and a musty smell. My mother would have hated rooms like that. She so liked light and air and pretty things. They were cold rooms also, and I knew this because my mother never took off her winter coat, wrapping herself in it and putting her hands deep into its pockets. She stood at the window and looked out over rooftops as it grew dark.

Or perhaps she was wearing her coat not only because of the cold. Perhaps she had just come in, or she had just put it on, she was getting ready to leave. Yes, she is watching for a car to arrive, and has put her coat on. Soon as she sees the gleaming black roof of the saloon car moving in the street below, she goes to the door, opens it, starts down the unlit stairs.

I kept on swinging until I felt cold and almost seasick, slowed then and dangled a foot to the ground, let it drag to and fro.

My mother is in the car now, coming to a bridge. Morning now, but so early that it is the same as twilight. The bridge is a steel one made of thick girders and there is a mist about it, between the Meccano girders. The car stops some way before the beginning of the bridge and my mother gets out of the passenger door at the back of the car and shuts it heavily, so that it makes a clunk like the door of the fridge, and walks away. The driver of the car is only an outline behind the windscreen. He keeps the car's engine running and its sound comes like a vibration through the mist to the huddle of people who are waiting on the other, near side of the bridge.

She walks briskly down the centre of the road. Her footsteps ring metallically on the asphalt. She has high heels, neat stockinged ankles, a thick coat that bells about her. She would appear to be dressed for an ordinary day in the city, a day's shopping or a visit to the doctor, not for this dawn walk across a steel bridge.

Once she is on the bridge the sound of her steps softens. There are no walls to harden them now but only open air. The river runs below, wide and cold and dark, but you cannot see it. You know it is there because of the mist that rises off it, that spills up about the skirt of her coat, that carries with it the raw waking breath of the land beyond the city.

And now the figure of another woman, slender and dark and darkly dressed, detaches itself from the group on the near side of the bridge and starts to cross in the opposite direction.

The swing was almost still now and I was cold, but the daydream held me. The notion that the two women might be exchanged, one for the other. Because one had a family and the other didn't have anyone and wasn't needed, and wasn't happy anyway. It didn't seem so unfair really.

I saw it happening: my mother coming closer; the back of the other woman receding, her red scarf a last point of colour in a grey distance, going wherever it was that my mother was coming from. Peter said that the spymasters were ruthless. Most of their agents were expendable but sometimes, if one was especially valuable to them, they would do things, even sacrificing one of the others, to get that agent back.

I left the playground and did not know what to do then so I went into the church. That seemed a good enough place to wait until the time when the lesson should be over. The churchyard still looked quite beautiful where it had not been trodden, snow still white between the graves and pelts of it coating some of the stones. Inside the church it was also white and just as cold, but there were dark oak pews to sit in, pews like boxes with tall backs, and doors at the side that closed a person in. I opened a door and latched it shut, and with its wooden walls about me I read the book that I had brought with me, that I had had the sense to put into my music case.

I read so hard that I did not at first hear the Vicar coming to lock up. When I did, when I heard the steps of a man walking up the aisle, I moved suddenly in a panic, and the music case fell to the floor.

'Well I never, aren't you cold?'

Of course I was cold, and my mind was all numb.

'I know who you are. You're Alec Wyatt's little girl.'

'I just came in, I was at my piano lesson. I was walking along. I just came in to see.'

'That's all right, my dear, you can come in here whenever you like. That's what the church is for. But you're lucky I didn't just lock the door and go away. I might have done that. You might have been locked in all night. I was just checking there weren't any birds inside. Sometimes a bird gets in, you see, and gets shut in, and flies against the windows and makes a mess everywhere.'

I knew the Vicar by sight. He turned up at school fêtes and things, and he was always gardening so that you saw him from the road whenever you went by the vicarage. He was bony and grey and a little bit awkward.

'I'll go home now.'

The Vicar smiled rather abruptly and brought out something from his pocket. It was a sixpence.

'Here, have this, I found it on the floor. I'm sure the church can do without it.'

I felt guilty taking the coin. I would put it into the collection in my own church that Sunday when we went to Mass.

It was just as it would have been those other times, if I
had gone those other times. The weather had not
changed. The sky was just the same. There was that same
static iron-greyness to everything in the day, to the morning when I had woken to it behind the curtains, to the
classroom and the journey home. Only there was a little
less snow. The road was clear and black. The hedges
showed bare where the snow had come off them. There
were some patches of pale grass now in the fields. And the
day seemed too long, wrong, because you should not have
had so much snow with that length of daylight.

'I haven't done any practice.'

She had a little cough. Perhaps she had been ill after all
and she hadn't minded about the missed lesson. She didn't
say anything about it. She just said well, let's ignore your
grades today, let's just start a new piece, shall we, and
turned to the shelves of music and started picking through
the books again, choosing and discarding. There was so
much music written there, whole days and years of music
to be played, but on this day, this particular grey day when

it was almost no longer winter but not yet spring, none of it suited. It had been played already, or it was too loud or too sad. There were only a couple of pieces that Sarah Cahn thought worth taking down and trying out, and she sat and played them through, and one was too loud and one was too sad, and I saw that she could not fix on anything and that she too wanted only to waste the hour away.

'This is something I play to arrange my thoughts. It's not hard, but it can be played very beautifully. You could play this if you tried.'

It was some Bach. Sarah Cahn went through it first and explained the harmonics, marking the score with the finely sharpened stub of a pencil, explaining how Bach could see all these patterns, what a mind he had, how clever he was.

'That's like Peter. He's clever too. He does Latin and Greek and he can make up codes and things.' Suddenly I wanted to talk, tell it all, ask if she knew, what she knew, if she was anything to do with it; knowing all the time that she wasn't, that there wasn't anything there to be found out.

She was demonstrating the piece and did not seem to hear. Not a piece of her face showed that she heard. The music was like fountains, crystalline, rising, falling, controlled. If only it was all like that, no words to anything. If you listened, closed your eyes, then opened them again and looked about, you saw the room more richly than before, the polish of the furniture, the glow of the lamps, of the glass on the shelves, the vividness of its lit colour. The woman at the piano was suddenly vivid again too, as if some veil, some dull greyness which had seemed only an extension of the greyness of the day, of the protracted late winter, had dropped away.

That was the last lesson I had with Sarah Cahn.

As soon as Peter came home for the holiday he wanted to go out to see how much snow was left. It's not how it was, I told him, it's nearly gone now, it's no fun any more. He did not like that, that things changed while he was away at school, that things could not just hold until he got back.

We went out on the Friday morning after our father had left for work. The air was still but cold and the sky was stark, the sun a hard luminous disc behind a thin screen of cloud. At the farm they were putting out new hay. The cows were still being kept in. Their black-and-white backs flooded out of the shed into the yard, spilling forward to the fresh hay. They would have to be kept in many weeks yet as there would be nothing for them in the fields.

We went up the hill first. We could not see far. The view dissolved too soon, without distinction between earth and cloud. There was only the valley, the bare roofs of the village, the road winding away, a hint of distance. Everywhere the white cover of the ground was worn thin, pricked through by dead stems, ribbed by the plough beneath. It was soggy walking on the tracks, easier in the open fields though we had to watch for dips where the snow still lay deceptively deep, and for the drifts against banks and hedges, though most of the paths were marked by now with the steps of walkers who had been before.

'How's Dad been?'

'Fine.'

He always asked that and I always gave the same reply.

'What've you been doing?'

'Nothing much.'

We started down, along round the backs of the houses. Peter led and I just went where he did.

There was always this adjustment to his coming home, the getting used to each other again, the waiting to see what sort of person he was going to be now that he had come back. Some holidays we were quite close. Others we had nothing to say to one another as if we had grown apart. At the top of the hill he stopped for a time so I stopped too and stood beside him. And when we went down, he went first and I came behind, and he bent and made a wet dirty snowball and threw it at me, and I made one too and threw badly, but Peter had already turned away and I think he did not see that I missed by miles as I always did.

It was habit to look in when we passed Mrs Cahn's house. I don't think that Peter had any particular intention. He was ahead of me and he looked casually down the slope, and then stopped.

'Hey, that's odd.'

The room was all moved round, the table pushed out of place. There was something on the cleared patch of floor before the cooker. Later I wondered if I had known from the first, if we had both known exactly what it was we saw, but really I think it was not clear, looking then. There was not much light, either outside or in. Nothing that morning was clear.

'It looks funny.' Peter had got up on the wall, sinking into a wet drift as he had done so, so that his jeans were all wet. 'I'm going to go and see.'

He jumped off and started down the slope towards the house. The covering of snow was still complete there and though the strip along by the wall was well walked, trodden so many times that it was a mass of tracks and holes, the stretch that ran down to the house was still clean and smooth so that each step Peter took in it showed clear.

'Don't, Peter.'

'Why not?'

'She'll see. She'll see you coming. She knows we come up here. She sees us go by, you know. She'll see you coming or she'll see your tracks later and then she'll know that we've been watching her.'

Perhaps I must have known, or I would not have panicked so.

'What's it matter?' Peter hesitated, stamped, churned up the snow at his feet. The air really wasn't clear. I couldn't see his face that clearly. The sun was there behind the mist and it was all a blind hard grey.

'Don't,' I said again. 'Just don't.' No why. Only, that I did not want him to go down there. 'Come back. Please, Peter.'

He just stood a moment.

'OK,' he said, and came back up.

'Race you home,' he said, and we ran down to the village, getting there heated and hungry, almost but not quite forgetting what we had seen. The awareness of it was there beside the awareness of the tracks that we were making, even as we ran: the tracks of that morning stretching out behind us, passing across those of other days, out of the newly smashed drift beneath the wall, past the marks of earlier outings, past the snowed-over crater where Peter had fallen before; the tracks of our running and the fresh, obvious track that Peter had just made on the cleaner snow of the slope above the house, a track that went a little way down the hill directly towards the house and then faltered and turned sharply back – evidence, if any were to seek it, that someone had gone there and walked down towards the exposed window and gone no further, and gone back and joined a companion and moved on and left the house to its secret.

I remember that Daphne Lacey had made shepherd's pie for lunch. Details like that lodge in memory among the big things. So I remember how she had forgotten that it was

Friday and that we were Catholics and did not eat meat on Fridays, and how I was glad not to have to have fish and told myself that God would think it was less of a sin to eat the meat than to be rude and refuse the food.

The pie had been made for Peter. She always did something special for him on his first day back. She cooked something he particularly liked, then bombarded him with questions and chatter and second helpings. It was kind. You could see that she was trying to bring him in, to make him feel at home. She was not as stupid as she looked. Only it was never quite easy, never relaxed. She could never settle a thought, as if settling a thought meant danger, as if looking fully at something might stop you altogether, freeze you in your tracks. Better to move on, flit on, keep warm. That's how you kept life going. Ask another question. How's school? Was it football this term? How did the scholarship exam go? When do you get the results? And Peter answered. He seemed bright and confident talking to an adult, the bright schoolboy that he was away from home, someone that I didn't really know, someone who surely couldn't have been out on the hill that morning. But he was brittle also, as if he, both of them, were actors in some clever play. School was fine, he answered, the exam was OK, and Charlie West had broken his leg.

They were only actors, hollow, speaking lines. I listened to them and their voices echoed as if I too were hollow inside. When they stopped talking even the silence had an echo.

'Are you feeling all right, Anna? You've hardly eaten a thing. You look a bit flushed. You're not coming down with a cold, I hope, not at the start of the holidays?'

Daphne Lacey put a hand to my forehead to see if it was hot. (Her hands were long and pale and slightly freckled, and clammy from the cream she used; she was always putting cream on them, taking off her kitchen gloves or washing them at the sink and standing there rubbing the cream into them before she put her ring back on.)

'I'm fine.'

'Perhaps you'd better stay in this afternoon, just in case. You were out an awfully long time this morning.'

'I'm fine,' I repeated, but did not argue. I thought of the kitchen down there, the stillness and the silence within it, the woman on the stone floor and the voices of two children that carry down from the hill and through the closed window. *No. Don't. Come back. Please.* The voices carry thinly across the distance. I saw suddenly what I should do. I should go out there again and check, without Peter. I should think of some pretext and go right up to the door and knock on it. Only I did not have the courage.

All weekend I tried to forget. My father was working outside for the first time in weeks. There was a tree that had come down in the blizzards and he took out his chainsaw to clear it and to cut the torn stump clean, cut it into sections and piled the big pieces for firewood, taking the rest down to the bottom of the garden where he might when it was drier have a fire. I stayed in and watched television. There was only the sport and an old film but I sat all afternoon huddled in a blanket on the sofa. The work made my father happy so that when he went past the sitting-room window he put his mouth and nose to the cold glass and made fish faces. His skin was smeared with dirt off the wood. Come on out, he mouthed. Later he came in and tried to persuade me again. He said that it was lovely outside, bright, it felt like spring at last. Even Peter was in the garden, working with him dragging branches to the site of the fire. We might go for a walk, go up the hill even.

'I'm not coming,' I said. 'I'm staying here.'

I would not go up there again until I knew that every last piece of the snow was gone.

'I can't help thinking about it,' Margaret was saying.

It was Monday. Margaret had come to clean and Mrs Lacey had come to talk to her and stopped to have a cup of coffee. Peter and I were in the hall and the kitchen door was open. Margaret was cleaning the silver. I had seen her get the things out earlier and spread newspapers across the kitchen table. The strong smell of the silver polish spilled into the hall.

'That poor lady, sticking her head in the gas oven like that.'

'She's dead,' Peter whispered.

It was such a small word once it was spoken. No more than a pebble dropping.

'She was lying there a day,' Margaret was saying, 'before they found her.'

His eyes looked at me like they could see inside.

'My sister Joyce was talking to one of the neighbours and she says they knew something was up when they didn't hear any piano playing all day Friday. They're right next door, see, and they'd hear the piano all day long, and in the nights too, sometimes she used to do that, they say some-times she'd get up and play in the middle of the night, like she'd never sleep, poor thing. Anyhow, this friend of hers comes round Saturday morning and can't get her to answer the door, though there's a light on, and goes to the other neighbours, the ones at the other side, and they went round the back and got in.'

How did they get in, if the doors were locked? They must have looked in the window, close to from the garden, and seen, and then they would have broken in, wouldn't they, for sure? I pictured it all. It was easy to make the picture because I knew precisely how it was laid out.

Peter was still staring at me.

'It wasn't me made it happen.' I spoke the words in my proper voice, loud and clear, so that they heard inside and stopped talking right away.

I helped Margaret clean the rest of the silver so that I did not have to be with Peter. I liked doing the silver anyway. I liked the pink polish, the way it clouded on the metal, the way it came off so easily and left the silver beneath so bright. I sat beside Margaret and polished the spoons one by one, polishing them with precision and laying them when they were done on their sides, the bowl of one nestling in the bowl of the next. I worked until the spoons were all done, teaspoons, dessertspoons, tablespoons, and Margaret had done the forks, then I went to fetch the cigarette box that was a wedding present to my parents,

208

and the little silver boxes from my mother's dressing table, and polished those, and the silver was cool and hard and bright.

Margaret hummed a pop song. She did not like to work in silence.

'You're quiet today.'

'Umm.'

'That brother of yours getting you down? Something he said, is it?'

'No. Nothing like that.'

I could see that she wondered if I had overheard. She knew it wasn't her place to tell me. She should have kept her mouth shut.

'Sometimes a person just doesn't feel like talking, that's all.'

Even when I was cleaning I could imagine things. I imagined the bridge again, in a mist. The mist was thick, so that you could not see from one end of the bridge to the other, so thick that the woman seemed to be walking only along the yellow tunnel of light that was made by the headlamps of the car that brought her, that waited now before the barrier on the near bank. She walked away with delicate steps that made no more than the slightest sound. You listened for the steps of the other woman who would come towards you, coming from the unseen distance; but she did not come. The dark woman walked on and the mist began to envelop her, taking away first colour – the red of her scarf, even the black of her coat – then form, until she had vanished entirely. After that, there was only mist, and the visible end of the bridge, and the girders slung into nothingness, and still the other woman did not appear. Now both of them were gone.

'You're sure everything's all right, love?'

'Of course. Why shouldn't it be?'

It wasn't my fault. You don't dream a person dead.

'Nothing I can help with?'

'No, nothing.' Airily. I heard my voice prim and posh, child to servant. I made up my mind that when they asked me I would not do piano any more. At my next school I would learn to play a different instrument. Clarinet, like Peter. Or flute. Flute was nice.

I went on with the polishing. I could see my face in the teapot, long-nosed like a gnome's in the distortion of its side. My fingers were grey with polish. The grey would wash off but the smell would stay for ages.

'Well, that's done now. That's a good job done.'

'Isn't there anything else? Anything more we can clean?'

'Not as I can think of.'

Margaret gathered the dusters together and put the lids back on, folded up the spread papers. 'You can help me put it all back if you like.'

Peter had been upstairs in his room all that time. I had heard him clumping around up there, shifting things, walking to and fro. When Margaret had gone he came down with a wastepaper basket full of exercise books and papers.

'What were you doing?'

'Just sorting,' he said. 'Things are going to be different now.'

'Aren't those your code books and things?'

'I don't want to leave them lying around.'

He went out to the incinerator in the garden, which was a big rusted metal barrel with holes in it, and made a fire and tore up the books and fed the papers to it sheet by sheet. He was out there for ages. I watched from the big window on the landing that had a view right across the garden. The incinerator was down by where they had been building the bonfire. We didn't use it much. It was there from the people who had lived in the house before and in summer it was almost hidden in a clump of stinging nettles tall as itself, but the clump was dead and flattened now where it had been heaped with snow, and the incinerator stood out very black with the orange flames rising from it.

I wondered if this meant that the game was over, if we could begin to forget about it now.

When Peter came back in he stood at the bottom of the stairs and looked up, waiting for me to say something.

'Well?'

'So you burned everything.'

'Yup.'

'So?'

Later, when I had the television on, he came into the sitting room and sat in the armchair.

'Don't keep looking at me like that.'

'I'm not looking at anything.'

'So look somewhere else.'

He was looking at the television but he wasn't watching it.

'Do you think the rest of her family died the same way she did? If she left them behind in Germany like you said, and came to England, then they probably died in the concentration camps. Then they were all gassed.'

'I don't know anything about it.'

'It was probably just the same stuff.'

'Shut up. I don't want to know.'

'The same kind of gas.

It's coal gas,' Peter was saying. 'It's made from coal and it's poisonous. It's a heavy gas so it gets you if you lie on the floor, like in the gas chambers where people climbed on top of one another to get the last of the air. Soon we're not going to have coal gas any more. We'll have natural gas and then people won't be able to kill themselves like that.'

'You could have done something if you wanted. You don't always need me to go along.'

'No, that's right. I don't, do I?'

This time our father thinks that we are old enough to know. He tells us before supper that Monday evening. He has something just heating up in the oven and he is wearing the apron he puts on for cooking. He makes the two of us sit at the table we have just laid and says it in a few straight words.

'There's something I have to tell you. Mrs Cahn died on Friday. I'm afraid they think she committed suicide.'

I like the plainness of the words. They steady your thoughts. Words like that can be arranged neatly like the knife and fork beside your plate.

'You're old enough now to know about things like this.'

Then like an afterthought he says, 'You should both say a prayer for her tonight. She had a very sad life. She lost all her family I think in the war, and she lost her husband after that.'

'Yes,' I say. 'She was very sad.'

That's it. Peter doesn't give any reaction at all. You might almost think that he has not heard. In the moment of silence that follows I feel tears coming, but coolly, without shudders, as if they are only water.

There was a girl on a train. Slight, dark, a little older than I was. The train was full of children.

There were only children on the train and they talked as long as the train was moving, but when it stopped adults came into the carriages and the children did not speak any more. The place where the train stopped was empty, in the middle of nowhere. The children clung on to themselves and the little cases they had with them, and repeated to themselves who they were inside and what they remembered until the train started going again and repeated it back to them.

Dad looks from one to the other of us, standing before us at the laid table, his apron on, his hands hanging down oddly spare. He always looks slightly out of place when he is cooking, slightly lost. Does it come to him in this moment what he had not said, before, what he can never bring himself to say?

4

Peter must have intended it from that same moment he decided to burn his things. It was a calculated operation, equipped and timed in advance. Nothing in his behaviour gave any indication, through those last couple of weeks of holiday, of what he had in mind. If there was anything different in him it was only that he seemed more grown-up, as if his resolution had separated him from us. He threw darts at his dartboard and he listened to Radio Luxembourg, and while he was doing this he put his plan together and worked out his route: from school to Oxford, to London, to Harwich, to wherever he meant to go from there. East.

'What are you doing?' I'd ask, and he'd say, 'Nothing,' and go back up to his room. Later he'd come down with his air rifle and go out and shoot things.

'Can I come too?'

'If you want.'

He went out with the gun under his arm and did not wait for me to put on my boots, so that I must run to catch up with him. He was going down through the orchard where the daffodils were trying to come up through the grass, late, and the old trees were grey and bare. There was a thicket of bramble and blackthorn, buds on it at last but nothing open, tracks of bared soil where animals went in between the stems. We waited there but nothing moved. Peter did not even put the gun to his shoulder.

'Usually there's lots of birds here.'

'Well, I can't see any.'

'It's like Dad says, the winter's done for them. They've all starved in the snow.'

'Then why are you trying to shoot them? If there are hardly any left, it's not fair to shoot them, is it?'

He started to walk on, away, not answering. Through a gap in the hedge, under a single sagging strand of barbed wire, into the field. No cattle there, but the indentation of a track along the field edge where the cattle walked last year. A couple of pigeons flew up from an elm, too quick for him. A crow scavenged something in the distance. He wasn't really trying. He held the gun under his arm most of the time, looked down at the ground and picked his way between the rough tufts of grass.

'Let's go back. I think it's going to rain.'

I could feel the first cold pinpricks of it, fine spots like mist.

We went through the gate now, down the track that passed the farm. There was an open barn, a bare stone barn with a corrugated iron roof and a few tractors and machines in it. At the side of it was a brick lean-to with a window and a padlocked door.

'Watch.'

The glass panes were black, with a sheen to them like water.

He put a pellet in his gun and aimed, and shot through the centre of the central pane. Silvery glass shattered and fell to the ground.

In the silence that followed the shot he cracked the gun open, put in another pellet, offered it to me.

'Want a go?'

'No.'

'Got to fire it now it's loaded.'

'I don't want to.'

He shot the pane to the right of the first one.

'Why are you doing that? It's not as if it's difficult.'

His look said that I should know, if I was tougher I would know, but I could see only the pointlessness of it.

He reloaded and shot again and again, with precision, until every pane in the window was gone, jagged edges of glass broken through to the matt blackness behind them, sharp shards on the darkening mud before the shed.

The rain was really setting in now. Further up the track, Richard's father was standing under the eaves of the cowshed, talking with another man.

'When they see, they'll know it was us.'

'Who cares?' Peter said.

He wasn't going to be there when they found out.

It was a sign of his cleverness that he left from school, not home. He even laid a false trail, told one of the other boys that he was going home, that he couldn't stick it at school any more. So they expected him at home when he ran away. The school called Mrs Lacey and she called my father and he came back from work, and for days there was someone in the house, all the time, in case he turned up or if he called, just my father at first, or Margaret or Mrs Lacey, but later it was a policeman. Mainly it was the one policeman, a stolid man who sat in the kitchen and smoked cigarettes and called me love, but sometimes it was others. Some of them wore uniform and some did not.

At first it was only my father who questioned me. Later, when Peter still didn't turn up, the police questioned me as well. Could I think of anywhere he might have gone, anywhere at all that he had mentioned? Even if it was only a hunch? No, I said, not at all. He didn't talk to me much any more. I didn't know anything he did. He hadn't said anything, ever. The denials mounted and spiralled until they made me feel guilty even when they were true. The police searched his room, where my father had searched already, searched the house, came in greater numbers and I heard that they were searching the countryside. That frightened me. That was what they did when children disappeared. They went out in lines, with dogs and sticks, policemen and soldiers and men like the men off the farm, and beat through grass and bushes and looked in ditches and ponds.

Usually when they did that, it was in the papers and on the News. So I turned to the News as the adults usually did – only they were not doing so now, they didn't bother. I looked in the paper and I watched the television at six o'clock. There was a real spy case going on. All the headlines were about a man named Profumo, and call girls, a smart brunette called Christine Keeler, who I didn't think was really very pretty. Nothing about Peter being missing. The world outside seemed far off, an entirely separate place. Or it was we who were separate: the house an island in space, and no one outside would be able to reach it, no one at all; not even Peter who'd got away.

In the end I told a policewoman, someone quite new, a young policewoman I had not seen before. She had come for a walk with me. I did not want her. I had tried to go for a walk alone but it appeared that I was not to be allowed to walk alone.

We went up the hill. It was a lovely day, all green, and the view blue in the distance and hidden in it were the people searching. There was the village below, and a police car on the road to it that must be coming to our house. Peter must be somewhere out there too.

I asked which direction Oxford was in.

It was easier that I had not met the policewoman before, not already lied to her, not evaded.

'I've had an idea. I just thought it, just now. I thought he might have gone there.' It was just possible that he had gone to Oxford because he thought that might be where our mother was.

I knew that he would hate me for telling.

*   *   *

Dad came to me. He looked so tired. I had never seen a man look so tired.

'It was only her coat. It wasn't her. It was only like her. I knew it wasn't really her.'

Once things were said you couldn't take them back. People took them and repeated them to one another and they were out of your control. It was the policewoman I told and now here was my father, asking more. They thought that I would tell him what I had not told them. They did not understand. I stuck to the story of the woman, the coat, the bus stop. Nothing more, and specifically, no mention of Mr Kiss or of the connection home. I'd watched the films. I knew the rules of interrogation. Talk if you must but disclose no more than is absolutely necessary. Then stick to your story, whoever's asking the questions.

A police car brought him back in the middle of the night. I heard it come. We had been told and were expecting it, and Dad had spoken to Peter on the phone. I had been sent to bed but lay there awake and waited, knowing by the light under the door that my father was waiting too, in the light downstairs, and the murmur of the television died, the notes of the national anthem with which the television closed down, and the clock struck twelve, and two – and I felt anxiety that I had fallen asleep and missed one, and lost count of the quarter-hours, and missed whatever might have happened in them. The car came quietly. The voices at the door were hushed and brief. I could imagine a sleeping or half-sleeping boy passed from one man to another, hear his steps as he was gentled up the stairs, his head resting against his father's shoulder, an arm about his waist, put into his bed. I did not get up to see him. I pretended sleep when Dad came into my room, afterwards, to check on me and tuck me up. Lie still; eyes closed, not scrunched, lips just open, breathing slow. I knew that the boy in the next room was awake as I was, alert to every sound and hating me.

'Why did you tell them?' he said.

Yet I had not led them to him. It was pure chance that he was found: a random check on a lorry in a Dutch port, an English boy hiding behind some crates. Easy enough once you have the boy to check him against the police register, even if he does not tell his name.

'I hardly told them anything. Just about the bus stop. And Dad drove me to Oxford with this policeman and we drove round and round, and I didn't even tell them which bus stop it was.'

'You told them anyway. Don't you see what that means?'

Too many words spilled out.

'I said it probably wasn't her. Just that we thought it might be. It was probably only the coat. They asked what coat, and I said it was the tweed one, that she got it in

223

Jaeger, that shop she used to go to, in Cheltenham, remember?'

'Don't you see?' he said again.

And, 'What if she's still here? What if they go and catch her?'

He had got to Hook of Holland. I took in the name of the place and pictured him there a hero like Scott at the Pole: Peter on a spit of land, the sea crashing about, a flag in the wind. But he did not seem like a hero. He had come home silent, brooding, shamed. He didn't speak to me or to anyone else. I remembered how it had been before and would have had that time back again, the spy game, the burnt ciphers, the suspicion, any of it. Then he could be an agent, not just himself. And there would be a story: Peter a secret agent returned from a failed mission, awaiting debriefing, temporarily incommunicado, guarding his secret like a wound. If it was a story there would be a way on. Something would happen. Wounds would heal. In stories something always happened next.

It was thought best, as Peter was to leave anyway at the end of that term, that he did not go back to school. He stayed at home, and for some days of the week or hours of the day someone was found to come to teach him. Dad took time off also, time which must have been meant for Peter, for contact, and yet he spent most of it in the garden.

It was very beautiful that year. I would come home from school and go out to find him and walk about it. Peter would be up in his room. I could see that he was there by the wide open windows but otherwise I would hardly have known it. Just beneath the windows and inside on the landing I could hear the thin sound of his transistor radio.

Dad mourned the losses of the hard winter. Many tender shrubs had died. Others had appeared to die but he had cut them back, almost to the ground, and suddenly fine shoots appeared, green or sometimes red-tipped, and he said, 'See, it wasn't so bad as all that. Things are still alive, underground.'

Where plants had gone or been cut away, spaces opened up that he filled with flowers. Some were from seeds he had sown early under cover knowing what was to come. They were light, airy things, simple flowers that I loved better than the shrubs. I walked round with him and he told me their names and I picked them and brought them into the house, poppies and cornflowers and snapdragons, and stocks that had tiny scented stars that opened in the evening so that the moths might come to them.

The roses also had names, Peace and Penelope and Masquerade. He let me take the secateurs and cut the dead heads. If you keep cutting them, he said, they'll flower all summer through. Where greenfly clustered along the tip of a new red shoot he rubbed his finger and thumb along the shoot and squeezed them off, wiping his fingers later on his handkerchief. (That I would not learn to do for years; it disgusted me so to see them squashed.) He inspected the buds, and if there had been rain and the buds had browned on the outside he pulled off the browned outer petals, gently so that he left the heart of the bud clean and intact.

Sometimes I was aware that Peter was watching from the window. He kept a pair of binoculars there on the sill, big old ones that some great-uncle had had in the Navy, and a round tin of air-rifle pellets, and the rifle itself propped up against the wall beside his curtain. Sometimes I saw the curtain pulled half over and the binoculars watching, sometimes the tip of the gun as if there was a sniper up there. He had a telescopic sight now: he would be able to see us as if he was close to, watch us blink and see our lips move as we spoke.

One day when I went to his room I found him kneeling at the window shooting the buds off the roses. Dad was mowing, walking to and fro on the lawn oblivious, the sound of the mower drowning the shots.

'How can you do that? He loves those things.'

'You wait. He'll pick them up and think they have some weird disease.'

And before I went out of the door I said, 'Where were you going, Peter?

'It was Königsberg, wasn't it? Or whatever it's called now it's Russia. You were going there.'

He didn't look at me but only aimed out of the window.

'Or maybe it was Berlin. It was silly anyway. You wouldn't have found anything.'

He turned. He didn't look into my eyes but only pointed the gun at my feet.

I got out quickly and heard the shot afterwards, heard the crack and heard the pellet hit the bottom of the door.

Then there was a day when it rained, and Dad took us to Oxford. It was raining when we got up and it must have been raining all the night as well. The water butt spilled over where the gutters emptied into it, the roses sagged on their stems with the weight of water in them and the lavender was dark like lead. I did not know if we went that day because of the rain which made it a bad day for gardening, or if it was because he had planned the trip already.

We had lunch on the way in a hotel along the road; red plush and a smell of smoke, the swish of cars going by in the rain, steak and chips, and then strawberries and cream, only the cream was piped and synthetic. He had not explained what we were going for and we did not ask, subdued by his look of mystery and by the rain which was constant and made everything slick and unreal like a film being screened. When we got to Oxford we did not go into the town centre but skirted it, crossing meadows limp with wet, turning almost out of the town again before we came to the gates. There was a long wall and then a gateway with high pointed railings. We saw the gravestones through the railings and knew where we were.

'I thought it was time you came here.'

Neither of us answered.

The gates were open but we parked outside and walked. Dad took his big black umbrella out of the boot of the car and put it up to hold over us but Peter had gone before him, the hood of his anorak down, hands in his pockets, out into the rain.

I would have held Dad's hand if it had not been holding the cane handle of the umbrella. I walked close. His steps were long and pressed me to go fast. (Always, even now, my friends comment on the length of my stride; they do not know how this began with stretching to keep up with my father.)

'Silly boy, he doesn't know where it is.'

Peter had walked up the main avenue to the centre of the cemetery, where there was a chapel and where smaller paths fanned off between the blocks of graves. The avenue was wide enough to take two cars passing, like a road; the other paths were narrower and would scarcely have fitted one. Peter was stopped some way ahead of us, beneath a tree, waiting in what little shelter it offered.

'Which way?'

'It's on the right, further up. I'll have to show you.'

So Peter had to fall in. He did not walk beneath the umbrella, not with us, never again quite alongside us, but lagged a few steps behind.

The stone was the simplest tablet possible: a flat rectangle the size of a big book, propped up on a stand like a book on a bookrest, and the name Karoline Wyatt on it and a date, and RIP, and just grass around it, flat, no indication of the grave or the shape of the hole that had been there. The grass was scattered with a few little wine-coloured leaves that had blown off the small tree beside it. I recognised the kind of tree; it was a dull sort of tree but it had small white blossoms in the spring, and it helped to keep the rain off while we stood.

'There. That's where she was buried.' The way he looked around him, he might not have been there before, casting his eyes about, taking it in, looking down the lines of graves as if he was studying all the little differences in them, the individual touches, the points and topknots and crosses and curves, the stone-framed rectangles of pebbles and pansies and coloured glass, the urns and vases. 'I always meant to bring you two here sometime. Perhaps it should have been before, I don't know.' He kept looking around as he spoke, so that I began to wonder if he was actually looking for something and what it might be that he was looking for. 'At the time it seemed best to keep it simple. We didn't want a fuss. A fuss wouldn't have been a good thing, would it, at the time?'

He had said we. Who was we? Henry and Madeleine, the Laceys? Who helped him fix it, without fuss? After all, there was only him to mind, and me, and Peter, who stood where the rain still dripped on him on the other side of the grave. Just the three of us, no one else. I thought this and we stood there, and for a time none of us said a word. A few paths further on, some distance off past two or three more blocks of graves, there was a man walking. He had on a hat and a raincoat, and walked as if he should have had a dog with him but there was no dog. And now that the rain was easing there was a gardener on one of the paths, pushing a barrow loaded with tools.

'Daddy, why didn't we bring any flowers? Why didn't you tell me, so I could have brought her some flowers?'

'Next time. Next time you can pick some flowers and bring them. This time you can just say a prayer.'

He stooped to clear the few strewn leaves off the grave. I did not see why he bothered to make it tidy if he had not bothered with flowers. He did not understand that I was really angry about the flowers. I could not forgive him for taking us there like that, as if it was so ordinary, and not telling me to bring some flowers. Had someone told him that too, that same someone who told him things should be done without fuss? Then I would not forgive him for doing what they told him, not ever. I tried to say a Hail Mary silently in my head but the words got tangled. The man without the dog was walking back the way he had come. A hearse had begun to drive up the main avenue, white and yellow flowers pressing against the length of its window. Three more black cars behind; people in them, not flowers. *Holy Mary, Mother of God, pray for us sinners now and at the hour of our death. Amen.*

We waited for the procession to go and then started back. The sky was lightening, luminous cracks in the clouds. When the sun came out it would all of a sudden feel like June again. But in these last moments of greyness

Peter muttered something in my ear. He brushed by me. He still had his hood up and his hands in his pockets with his elbows out so that he jabbed my side. I didn't catch his meaning until he had gone on a few yards ahead down the path. He said something about Harry Lime. The name took a moment to register.

Harry Lime was the man in a film we'd seen on a Sunday afternoon.

People went to Harry Lime's funeral but he wasn't dead.

Peter was walking away like Harry Lime's girl did in the film, walking down the wide aisle between the graves. He was walking on, away, and he would not look up even if I went alongside, even if I were to go past him and call.

Harry Lime was in Vienna, of course. *The Third Man* was set in Vienna, not Berlin. I used to see my parents meeting on the wet cobbles of a shadowy Vienna. Even now, coming to Berlin, I must remind myself of what is true.

A tram line passes the hotel room in Kastanienallee. When I wake I hear the rain first and then the tram. I know the sound as it comes to a stop just across from my window, the soft rush as it goes on. Even if I have not lived with the sound of a tram before it is one that is familiar and full of associations as it has been heard a hundred times in films: long raincoats and cigarette smoke and fleeting encounters; my father and mother there as characters in a story.

'You know where we met, don't you? It was in 1947. I'd been in Berlin six months, interpreting, and this young German girl came into the office one day and it was your mother.' Dad was driving home after we'd been to the cemetery. I sat in the front, Peter slumped and sullen in the back. He was talking to me but he was trying to deal with the problem of Peter. I could see that. It was easier to have me in the front and address his words to me but really he was speaking to Peter. We were driving along a straight high ridge over the top of the Cotswolds. I used to love that stretch of road. The land fell away from it in a wide valley like the Promised Land in my illustrated Bible.

'She didn't have anyone. There were people in Berlin who had no family, no home, nothing but their names, and she was one of those. You have no idea how it was in Berlin then, how destroyed it was. I've got some photographs somewhere, I don't think I've shown them to you, have I? Well, I'll show them to you sometime. They're not much, just houses reduced to rubble, sometimes a wall standing with a chimney in it, or the front of a house, an apartment-block façade and there's only sky through the windows. When you look at them you have to multiply them in your mind, think of whole streets, districts, a whole city like that, great mounds of bricks and paths going through where there had been straight wide streets, and people were living in this, living right in the middle of the ruins. They had tidied them and stacked the bricks, and marked bits off and made shelters. Some of them lived in the cellars that were left when houses were destroyed above, and climbed out when you didn't expect to see anyone, they'd come up suddenly like ghosts, pale from under-ground, or if the weather was good they would have cooking stoves outside, and sit around, all neat and tidy sometimes, families with little girls in plaits, sitting on chairs among the bricks eating their food.

'Anyway, your mother wasn't one of those. She'd found an apartment somehow in a partially damaged building. The rooms were fine but the front of it was shot up and the windows were gone so she had put paper across them. Just her there. She didn't have any family and I don't think she knew anyone. She was meant to be sent out to the countryside. That was what they did with most of the German refugees; they were all sent to different towns and villages, but she had managed to get to Berlin and stay there on her own, and she spoke English and was useful, so we found work for her. Your mother was lucky. There were thousands about like her. And there were a million others besides Germans: French and Italians and Poles and Lithuanians and Czechs and what-have-you, who'd been forced to work in Germany during the war or somehow ended up there, and some of them were still in camps and some were just milling around. Most of them were trying to join up with their families again, if their families were alive and if they could trace them, and get back to wherever it was they came from, and some who came from the East, like your mother, didn't want to go back. They'd moved the boundaries, you see, and pieces of Poland and Germany became Russia, and other pieces of Germany became Poland, and it was all a great muddle. A lot of people wanted to go on to Britain or America, somewhere new, because they thought they would find nothing left where they came from or because they were scared of the Russians or because they thought they would do better in the West.'

'Like Harry Lime's girl,' I said.

'Who?'

'Harry Lime's girlfriend in that film. She was all alone, and she needed papers and Harry got them for her.' Anna Schmidt, she was called. Another Anna.

'Well, yes,' he said. 'I suppose it was a bit like that.'

A pause then. The sound of the car. I hadn't really understood why Anna Schmidt needed the papers so badly. It came to me that my mother looked a bit like Anna Schmidt; and the actress who was Anna Schmidt looked a bit like Hedy Lamarr. They all looked a bit the same.

Peter spoke for the first time since we were in the cemetery.

'How long did you know her, when you got engaged?'

'Oh, not very long. A few months. She came in the winter and we were engaged in the spring. We got married pretty much as soon as we were allowed.'

'What had she been doing, before?'

'She moved around, from place to place. It was a chaotic time. As I told you, there were a million people on the move.'

'Why didn't she look for her family? She should have been looking for her family.'

'She didn't have any family left.'

'How did she know, if it was all such a muddle? How could she be so sure?'

His questions came from the back of the car like a series of shots, one after the other, each one becoming a little closer and more hostile. The car slowed. We came to a roundabout and turned off it in silence. And that was the

236

end of the story. I suppose Dad thought that time would heal. That's what people would have told him: leave the boy, let him be; he'll get over it, he just needs time. So he put the radio on and we listened to the soothing voices of the Home Service all the rest of the way home. He didn't attempt to go back to the subject later. I could see why. It wasn't the kind of conversation you could start up again. It was the sort of conversation that could happen only in transit, in a car, when you didn't look at one another but only at the road.

His photos are nothing special. I have them with me so that I can attempt to identify their sites: faded shots of the River Spree, of young Russian soldiers in some relatively intact street, of a train of refugee wagons passing a spanking new Russian memorial. I imagine he took his pictures with the same little Brownie that I remember, that he kept for years. They are small, faded, vague, not nearly so good as those that are reproduced in books, but they have a particular value. They have meaning because I know who took them, because they speak to me directly as the extensions of a lost memory. These things my father saw. When he died and I cleared his house I brought the album home. At some point, when the occasion arose, I showed it to my daughter. That was Berlin just after the war. Where your grandparents met. But my daughter perceived them only as history. Where I was still implicated, she was detached. She looked through the pictures with an objectivity which was the difference between history and memory.

The old postcards they sell in Berlin will mean as much to her: the defeated city, the Reichstag without its roof. I have bought some to send home. I shall write them this morning before I catch my train. I shall get to the station in good time so that there is no worry, and then I can sit somewhere and have a last coffee and write my cards. There is one of a springtime crowd in the open-air cafés of an Unter den Linden without limes. I shall send her that one. *Funny to think that your grandparents could have been there, in that picture.*

So many faces there: the faces of Allied soldiers, bombed-out Berliners, camp survivors, the displaced from all of Europe, mingled beneath the spring sun. They wear uniforms and smart city clothes and some things that are almost rags, and some of these outfits are worn as surely as skin and others with doubt as if the wearer had only that moment stepped into them. So many stories there, and my mother's story is just one of these, the story of a girl who is one of eight million driven out from eastern Germany, coming alone to Berlin, making her way, getting out. The story will have certain standard elements of tragedy – it is a story of war, after all, of war and defeat with all the variable probabilities of bombing, loss, flight, rape – and particular features at which I can only guess: some special quality of toughness or of marvellous luck in its protagonist, who came a refugee and left with a British officer husband and a silver fox coat.

In the films the Ostbahnhof was a sinister place, the station in the East a connecting point to the West and thus a place of surveillance, of whispers and observing eyes, where a raw-faced soldier in an ugly olive uniform stood at the edge of the platform sighting his machine gun along the painted yellow line. Its present reality is innocuous: up stairs, raised above the streets, a dozen grey platforms; isolated figures on them, walking, standing, fumbling at ticket machines.

This first train is headed for the Baltic coast. There are few passengers on a wet Monday in April. In an hour I will get off and change for Poland. I have a window all to myself and watch the landscape, looking for whatever details define it beneath the rain. The city has been quickly passed, the order of the massive Communist blocks randomly broken down between factories and allotments and new housing, giving way to land that is wide and low, that rolls in long undulations, showing green with new wheat beneath the greyness of cloud. It would be similar to parts of eastern England, only there are lakes, and the long rectangles of arable fields are broken up by rambling stretches of forest, dense forest that is used for hunting, with wooden towers for shooting deer set up in clearings and in fields close to the forest edge. Every so often a group of wind turbines stands white and pure on a rise in the land. So this is the place that was East Germany.

The station where I must change trains is a small one. A handful of other passengers are making the same connection. Two youths who look like students. An old woman and her daughter. The others travelling separately, two other men, a lone girl in a bright-yellow mac. The colour is the most distinctive thing in the journey. It goes ahead of me along the open platform to where the new train is waiting, enters the far end of my carriage. Along the corridor inside I catch a glimpse of yellow passing into a compartment.

In Poland the rain has eased off. I must have been dozing for a time. There is more forest now than farmland outside the window. I take a small bottle of water from my bag. The water is fresh and clean, and my mouth was dry after sleep. I begin to enjoy just the sense of travelling, the flatness, the anonymity of it.

There is a small boy in the compartment. For most of the journey he has sat quiet beside his mother but now he is bored and wanders between our legs. His mother with a tired gesture pulls the door shut before he can go out into the corridor, pats the seat and tells him to come and sit down again. But he doesn't. He stands before me and stares, his hot hand on my knee. Why does he come to me? He comes like a cat selecting the person in a room who shows least interest. I do not easily make contact with strange children. I am too shy, I suppose, too conscious. Wary of what a child might see.

This boy's look is blank, without awareness. He is not an attractive child. The other passengers, another young woman and a middle-aged man, watch as I say hello to him in English.

'I am sorry,' says his mother, scolding him in his own language. 'He is bothering you.'

'No,' I say. 'Not at all.'

'You are English?'

'Yes.'

'Where are you from?'

'London.' It is not true but it is easy to say. I have spoken to people enough to understand that they like it if I come from London. What does it matter here who I say I am?

'My cousin is working there.'

Most of the Polish people I meet will have a cousin working in London. The others in the carriage observe the conversation but do not speak. Probably they understand what I am saying. They too will have cousins in London.

'Where are you going?'

'Gdańsk.'

'Tourist?'

'Yes.'

The boy loses interest and the other woman offers him a biscuit. A conversation starts in Polish.

I saw Peter shortly before I left. He happened to be in London on business so I went up for the day and met him for lunch. It was probably a mistake that it was lunch. Dinner might have been more relaxed. Peter was in a suit and the restaurant was full of businessmen, and every time he looked at his watch I was aware that he had a meeting to go to afterwards.

He didn't eat much either. He said that he had to eat too many dinners on business trips and only wanted something light. So we had salads, no wine, and the table seemed too empty to fill the time.

Peter has done well, keeps well. In Hong Kong, he said, he keeps fit, swims, goes to the gym, sails at weekends.

'That's good,' I said. 'I should do more exercise. I don't seem to do much nowadays apart from a bit of gardening.'

His wife, his girls were all fine, though I don't know if he would tell me if they weren't. My family were fine too. The news is done with fast, in these sporadic meetings, relayed over too great a distance, like telegrams used to be, every word counted, counting for more than itself, others left out in the spaces between. Another day I might have tried to spin it out but this time I wanted the preliminaries over so that I could tell him about the trip I had planned.

'You won't find anything.'

'But at least I'll see. I've never seen any of those places.'

'Berlin's worth the visit. There's some stunning new architecture, and wonderful art. You'll enjoy the art. But you don't want to go to Kaliningrad. It's Russia. you know.'

'Of course I know. I've got my visa, haven't I?'

'But are you sure it's safe?'

Just fifteen minutes together and he had me on the defensive. Peter knows more than me. He always knows more. The old patterns remain.

'Why don't you just take a nice holiday? Come and see us. You've never done that.'

Peter doesn't look one quite in the eye. Or if he does, his look passes on too quickly. There are layers of reserve in him, with me at least. I know too much. I know who he used to be.

We talked on, stilted, skirting things. We had coffee. He asked for the bill. The movement seemed to make it easier for me to speak, that we were turning in our chairs, that the waiter was clearing the cups away.

'I saw something odd in the paper, just the other day. An obituary for Istvan Kiss, did you see? He died. He was famous after all.' (And real. I did not say that but the thought hung there between us, the whole story that we had never mentioned, the knot of words and adult figures in some deep pit of memory, that we evade, that we have evaded all our adult lives, that we have never once unravelled even to excuse ourselves, to say that we were only children, that it must anyway have been too late, that there was nothing that we might have done.)

Peter was getting his credit card from his wallet. It was a smart wallet, lots of cards in it. The waiter stood ready to take his payment.

'I saw him play once, didn't I ever tell you? Years ago, when I was working in Boston.'

So he had not forgotten either. He had forgotten no more than I, for all his smoothness. And I answered as smoothly, covering it over.

'No, I never knew. Was he good?'

'Very good. He played a Bach concerto. He was superb.'

Then the waiter was gone and there was an opening between us.

'Goodbye, Anna. Look after yourself in Russia. And tell me if you do end up finding anything, won't you?'

Poland first. I check the time. We will be at Gdańsk soon. It is necessary to gather my thoughts before arrival, not only book and bags and coat. Where to go. How to get there. It looks bleak outside even though there has been no rain here. I will need to wear my coat, and besides, if I wear the coat I will have less to carry. (For two weeks I have more luggage than Sarah Cahn had for the rest of her life.) The man opposite picks up my scarf from the floor and hands it to me. It must have fallen when I took the coat down from the luggage rack. He says something all in Polish but his gestures explain: no hurry, calm down. This is only Gdynia. Gdańsk will be the next stop, or possibly the one after. He is a squat middle-aged man with stubby fingers and scarcely a neck, but his face is kinder and more expressive than you would expect. So I must sit a while longer, hot in my coat with my suitcase crowding the footspace and another bag on my lap.

An anxious moment squeezed in the corridor before the door, and then I am out on the platform. In Poland. I join the flow of people off the platform and down into an underpass. That must be the way out, but I cannot ask. Coming to a new country like this one feels suddenly without voice as well as language, without identity. There is the coat again, the bright yellow of it, and the wearer who is a Polish girl with hair of a synthetic copper colour. Again I find myself following her, through the crowded tunnel beneath the station, lifting my suitcase up the steps that emerge into daylight, crossing the road towards the gables and spires that mark where the old town is, that are the rebuilt buildings of Danzig. My coat begins to feel too warm now. The wheels of the case snag on the cobbles. I shall stop in a café. I shall stop a moment before finding my hotel.

Next morning I ask the girl at the reception desk for directions out to the Vistula lagoon.

'There's a resort called Krynica Morska,' she says. 'But it's not the season. There'll be no one there.'

There's one bus a day this time of year. It goes in the morning and stops a while, and comes back in the afternoon.

It's a bleak journey, out of the city and through the flatness of the estuary. Square drained fields, ditches, old willow stumps like men's thumbs pointing at a huge dull sky. The sandbar is not as I imagined it, not all a shifting line of dunes but sand pinned down by trees, a thin forest of pines along a sixty-kilometre spine of land between Vistula and Baltic. Krynica Morska looks as deserted as the girl said. The bus stops. The driver puts his feet up on the dashboard and lights a cigarette to begin his two-hour wait. I get out and walk. There were only a couple of passengers besides myself, locals who disappear soon into a side street. The road runs on along the sandbar with the rushes and the still water of the lagoon close on one side, and on the other, a dense belt of pines. The beach must be hidden beyond these, the evidence of its existence in the strings of deserted summer hotels and campsites whose names are posted along the road, but it is hard to choose a turning and I go on a long way until the road begins to narrow, and then I turn back and take one of the paths in between the trees to find the sea.

It is further to the sea than I had thought, the path crossing a succession of dunes and hollows. I had not thought that the walk would be so long or so monotonous. Yet to those who escaped this way in the war these trees and dunes would at least have offered some kind of shelter, places to huddle after the awful exposure of the ice. When I come out at last on to the beach the wind is cutting. Out in the open that January it must have been sharp like blades. The band of pale sand runs for miles, a line into the far distance, and the waves roll on to it in angry white bars off a hard and slate-green sea.

It is too cold to walk far, too hard in the wind, a futile effort anyway as the beach goes on unchanging and the waves relentlessly repeat themselves. Back among the pines the quiet closes in. There is the roar of the sea and the wind on one side of the bar, and the silence of the lagoon on the other. This is where they passed. I feel that I am walking through a vacuum, timeless. I imagine the scene as I have read of it, the noise, the chaos, the shouts of soldiers, the children's cries, the mothers' words to the children that are brusque words of command and encouragement spoken like words to an animal. The horses, carts in snow, the retreating tanks forcing through them. The trampling, the debris of those who have gone before, the dead and the stragglers, who also have become like debris. The body of a woman who died as her baby tried to feed from her frostbitten breast. I wonder how it would mark a person, if they saw such things.

There is time before the bus leaves to warm up in the one café that is open. Just a teenage girl behind the bar, a boy talking to her, no one else there, and she brings out hot soup that must be their own. I catch sight of myself in a mirror: a lonely foreign woman whose face has been whipped by the wind. No one can know whether the shine on my cheeks is the result of wind or tears.

Before leaving home I got out all the pictures I have of my mother and spread them before me. I looked closely at each one as if I might find in them some indication of her experience. I cleared the kitchen table and arranged them all one afternoon. That was my mother as she was when she married my father; just after she came to England; before Peter was born; then when he was born; then with myself; at home, as we were growing up. I put them into chronological order as far as I could, putting the loose ones beside those from albums, as if some narrative would come from them if only I could put them all together.

There was a studio portrait that must have been a favourite. There was a black-and-white print of it and a hand-coloured one, of my mother smiling to camera, head a little tilted and resting on one hand, hair and face flatteringly lit from above. A face and pose entirely of that time, like a million other women in engagement photographs or on the shiny pages of magazines. I took the two pictures from their frames as if that would make them more real, and found the stamp of the photographer on their backs: *K.L. Haenchen, Atelier für Fotografische Bildnisse, Berlin W15, Bayerischestrasse 31.* So these were the photos I had to put at the very beginning: the first extant photographs of my mother, and they were the most polished and perfect of all.

My daughter is around the age she was then, in the first pictures. Nineteen, and seeming so sure of herself that it is like an armour about her through which I feel I cannot reach.

'What was your mother like?' she asked. She picked up the pictures one by one, scrutinised them, put them down, jumbled my arrangement.

What could I say? I had the pictures there before me, and all I could see in them was a smile, a prettiness, a bland image of post-war New Look woman.

'I think she looked a little bit like you do. See, you have her eyes, the line of her brow.'

'But besides that. Who was she?'

'A mother.'

'You can't just say that.'

'Not when you're the age you are now. But you can when you're eight. They're just mothers then, aren't they?'

'Then work it out. What kind of person she was.'

As if you could. As if I hadn't tried.

'I don't know. I simply don't know. It's harder than you think.'

That made my daughter angry.

'That's you all over. You give up on things. It's like you don't really want to find out.'

'That's what I'm doing now, isn't it?'

'Well, it's taken you a long time.'

I didn't see what cause she had to be angry with me.

1957 or perhaps it is '58 or '59. Helen Kroger is home doing the dishes. Christine Keeler is still at school. My mother puts on her face in the yellow-curtained bedroom. I am there beside her, watching. I often do that. It is one of the things I like to do. The dressing table is one of those kidney-shaped ones that were the fashion at the time, covered in the same yellow fabric as the curtains, and with a glass top on which are laid out the various bottles and jars my mother uses, powder compact and lipsticks, hairbrush and hand mirror and the collection of little silver boxes. Pressed beneath the glass are half a dozen photographs of myself and Peter at various ages, and a couple of the whole family and of Dad, but none from any time before Peter was born.

It happens every morning, just the same, only the shade of lipstick may vary, ever so little, to match what she is wearing.

'She was attractive, everybody says. She dressed well, put a lot of effort into her appearance.'

'Come on, Mum. There must be something more than that.'

I can speak only of surfaces.

'I think she was quite' – hard to choose the word – 'distant. Not at home, at home with us she was warm, but outside. I don't know if she had any friends. I don't remember any.' I do not know about her friends but I do know how she smelled, that close smell of scent and face powder that was the smell of her hug.

'Probably that was because she was German.'

'Perhaps.'

My daughter offered to come with me. Why don't you wait until the university term's over, then we can go together? We'll go and see where she came from. Find the old ancestral roots.

That wouldn't work, I thought. I said I had the trip just about booked, that arrangements had been made that couldn't be changed. Perhaps that was a mistake. Perhaps I should have had her come. It would have brought us closer. But I couldn't do it. I couldn't have her know how thin the story was.

Her face shows at three angles in the mirror. Brown hair falling back in smooth waves. Glassy skin, blue eyes. A look that people say is a little like Hedy Lamarr.

She leans forward to get a closer view.

'I am beginning to get wrinkly,' she says, but lightly, and when she smiles I see that tiny wrinkles do show about her eyes. 'I shall have crow's feet when I am older.'

And she puts foundation on, stretching her face as she does so and smoothing it with her fingertips, rubbing with a light circular motion beneath the eyes. At that age I have a literal ear for words. Crow's feet fill me with horror.

She brushes her hair, backcombing just a little, fixes the waves with tortoiseshell combs to the side of her head.

'It's a pity,' she says. 'You have fine hair like mine. My mother had hair like that. Whatever you do, it flies away or frizzes the moment you step outside.'

There are a few facts like that that come through from these morning rituals, to remember and hold on to later.

*   *   *

252

'What was it like,' I asked one time, 'where you lived when you were a child?'

'Not like this.' My mother looked about her and smiled, and the German accent was noticeable in what she said then, perhaps because what she said drew attention to her foreignness. 'Nothing like this, this English countryside. It was a proper city. There was a castle and a cathedral on an island in the river, and bridges and big streets and churches with spires. Our house was tall, five storeys. We lived in an apartment up lots of flights of stairs. My grandmother lived in the apartment above us, another flight up. We were lucky that way, having her there. I used to go and see her on my own. I was special to her because I was the youngest and because I was named after her.'

'Then she was called Caroline.'

'Who?'

'Your grandmother was called Caroline like you.'

'My grandmother?' Her voice hesitant, blank a moment as if she must remember. 'No, not Caroline, not the English way. Ka-ro-li-ne. In Germany they say it differently, with another syllable at the end.'

'Tell me something else.'

'What about?'

'About where your grandmother lived.'

'Well, let me see.' She picked up an eyebrow pencil and bent to the mirror, arched her eyebrows to draw them darker. 'Let me think. My grandmother's apartment was more exciting than ours. It was smaller than ours but it was crammed with funny old things, pictures and ornaments and furniture. And it had an attic. There were some windows there, like eyes right up in the roof. I used to go up there and look out from the roof and see all the city underneath, and see the ships.'

'Can we go there one day?'

'There's nothing there. From what I hear, it's all destroyed.' She put the little pencil down in a dish and took up her lipstick.

'There must be something we can see.'

She rolled her lips against each other and then opened them and leant forward again to check there was no smudge of lipstick on her teeth.

'What earrings do you think I should put on?'

And I understood that the past was closed and that a woman put on the present like her make-up, like her earrings, in the morning for the day to come.

There are different kinds of memory, conscious and unconscious. There are memories that the conscious mind goes over repeatedly, that are recalled, observed, caught like a snapshot of the time, and oneself in it, one of the figures in the picture. Memories like these become like history, fact-filed for recall, detached from emotion. But there are others that come back without conscious thought and that are experienced again, more or less vividly, like dream versions of themselves. These cannot be controlled and can come at any moment, and catch you unawares and remind you of things that you had forgotten you had ever known. Then there are memories that seem to run like a film, smoothly overlaying all the others, that have such shape and form that you suspect that they are inventions and may have created themselves, and within them your own identity even begins to slide and fade, and is liable to change as in a dream.

I had the illusion that if I collected all that I remembered together, like the photographs, if I worked it all through, I would come down to some consistent truth to set against the realities of history and place. But the memories change and slip and multiply, the more I follow them. They become flat and glossy like the photographs, like film, like glass, so many shiny surfaces, all of them sliding one above the other. And there's no breaking through, nothing beneath.

Sometimes my mother would dress me up. She would let me choose a dress, some light, silky thing that could be draped and tied with a sash. She would help me put it on and then find the sash and tie it round my waist, pulling the skirt up and folding it under so that it would not fall beneath my feet and make me trip. You can let it go at the back, she would say, let it trail like a bride, but at the front it must be shorter, and you must lift it up with your hands, like this, so, when you run or go upstairs. I felt grand in the dress and asked if I could wear lipstick, and my mother would bring the lipstick and kneel before me to put it on, very carefully, and as carefully I would go to the mirror and press my lips together like she did. My mother went to her jewellery box and found beads that she wrapped round and round my neck, held back my hair and tied a scarf in a turban over it, and when she was done she stood back and told me to turn this way and that so that she could admire the effect.

I was in disguise.

I went into the garden where my father was working. I held up a sweet cigarette (you bought them in packets of ten at the village shop, sweet white sticks with a reddened end like fire). Told him I was Hedy Lamarr.

I get my first sight of Kaliningrad through a smeared taxi window. A big Russian city, bigger than I had imagined. No castle here now but the cathedral on the island is at last being restored, some sixty years after its wartime destruction. The city centre that was once dense with tall streets and spires has been scraped away and replaced with a vast housing estate of huge decrepit apartment blocks and littered public spaces, and roads wide as runways. The taxi does not slow as the driver in his few abrupt words of English points out the cathedral and the brutal high-rise of the half-constructed Palace of the Soviets, exposed in the barren space. It does not slow for an old woman who pushes her shopping – or perhaps it is her produce – in a handcart across the road. I feel a sudden panic. This cannot be an official taxi. It is clapped out, filthy, with torn seats and a bad smell. No meter. It was so hard at the station to tell what was what. I am no good at travelling like this. I do not trust this driver. I hardly noticed his face when I got in but his neck from behind is thick and there are greasy strands of hair on his collar. I should not be here. This place is Russia. Its people are Russian. What can it have to do with me?

He does at least bring me to the right hotel. He asks for twenty US dollars. I give it to him. I have no idea what the correct fare should have been.

I check into a small dingy room on an upper floor, leave my bags and go out straight away. I have a sketchy tourist map from the hotel desk. It does not tell me much but there is at least some writing on it in a script that I can read. The hotel is on Prospekt Mira. I take my bearings, walk on down the street. So long as I stick to the main streets that are shown on the map I shall be able to find my way back.

I don't know which way to go. It is a big city, that much I saw from the taxi. Prospekt Mira seems to be a major shopping street. None of the buildings seem to be residential. Their entrances bear a confusing mass of signs for the little businesses that go on behind the windows, floor by floor. Some have old façades but most are post-war, all of them uniformly blank beneath their coating of dirt. The traffic is heavy, the noise of it and the fumes. I walk where the place takes me. One thing about being alone is that it leaves you free to drift. No discussion about where you're going, no explanations, no naming. No family to hold you back. (Was that what Peter found when he went away and left us? Why he could not return?)

I should have got myself an old German map before I came here, so that I could compare it with the Russian street plan. There is a bridge crossing a deep ravine, a green cleft in the city that would be lovely if the trees in it were not hung with windblown litter. The entrance to the zoo is here, and a café with a decorative awning and an upstairs terrace, but the tea comes in a plastic cup and it is too cold to sit for long.

Her house went up five storeys. Inside were many flights of stairs. In the attic, a window like an eye.

She told the truth: there is nothing here. It was all destroyed, if not in the war then in the years after, blown up, torn down, bulldozed, levelled, so that the entire centre of the Prussian city was erased. The Russians did not just take the city and rename it, they systematically destroyed its identity, made it into another place altogether. This is not a city out of her childhood, but out of mine. I come to a vast open square. The scale and the architecture are Stalinist, heroic banners stretched across the façades of municipal buildings proclaiming sixty years of *Kaliningrad Kultura*. This piece of Russian I can decipher. This is the Russia that I imagined, that we all used to imagine once. I cannot help a wary look behind me, at a man in a leather jacket, a head that seems to turn away too fast from my eyes, a cigarette stubbed out too deliberately on the pavement. Perhaps this also is something that I came for.

It's getting dark. I walk back. I have come further than I realised, but at least I am not lost. The traffic is heavy down this street, the noise of it and the fumes. People walk fast. They are city people, modern Russians, new Russians; people in leather coats, high heels; looks from the Calvin Klein posters; women with catwalk struts. The poor are grey shadows beside them, pushed aside as if there is no connection to be made between new Russians and old. People are remaking themselves, in this ugly remade city. And I pass them all, mute, fearful, quite out of place.

I eat in the hotel restaurant. Its blandness is a relief. I shall spend the evening here. I shall not go out again. The menu is dull, cosmopolitan – pasta, Waldorf salad, club sandwiches – as neutral as the decor of the room. No wonder that it is almost empty. There is only a man with a briefcase in the far corner, and myself, and an elderly German couple who come to sit at the next table. They talk to me. I have barely talked to anyone for days. The man speaks a slow and deliberate English. It is simple, soothing to me in my state of mind.

'You are not German, are you? No, English, I thought it. And what are you here for? You can't be a tourist, surely? There is nothing for a tourist here.'

There is something oddly stilted to his speech, a halt that occurs now and then at the beginning of a word or phrase, as if he has trouble with it, with a syllable that he cannot sound, as if he has some impediment or suffered a small stroke perhaps and speech no longer flows as easily as it once did; perhaps he talks to reassure himself that his voice is really there. He has white hair, far receded, a long face, eyes a clear blue. His cheek is a little hoary where he has not shaved quite perfectly. His wife watches beside him and does not speak but nods now and again so that it would appear that she can understand the English.

'I was born here,' the man says. 'Here in Königsberg. I left in December 1944 when I was eight, with my mother and my older sister and my younger brother, who at the time was only two years old. We went by train to Danzig, crossing the Vistula when it was still possible, when the railway bridge was still there. My father and my older brother did not follow us until later. My brother and a friend came by boat from Pillau. My father made the walk across the Frisches Haff. I come back now. I came as soon as it was possible to come here in the Nineties, and I have come back again six times. This time we are here for a week, my wife and I, though she is not from here, she comes from the Ruhr.' (There is a care to the way his wife watches him, as if she is indulgent because of the frailty in him. This to her must be no holiday at all.) 'Even before 1990 I was trying to come here. It was a closed city, you must know, under the Soviets. It was impossible for Germans or any other foreigners to come here. I was writing to my president, from Frankfurt, asking for him to help me.'

'I came for the same sort of reason you did,' I say. 'To find out about my mother.'

Sometimes the click quite goes from his voice and he relaxes and his speech comes easily.

'Today we went to the sea. Where we used to go for four weeks at a time in the summer. It was always beautiful there at the sea, even when in Königsberg it was grey. Like now, like it has been today. It is grey here today but there was sunshine by the sea. You could do that, take a taxi and go to the sea. I can give you the number of my driver if you like, he will give you a rate for the day, it is not so expensive to have a driver here. I showed my wife how to find small pieces of amber. You can find them there, if you look in the sand, tiny pieces of amber like these.' And he brings out a clean white handkerchief from his pocket, and folded inside it are specks of yellow amber.

'My mother told me about the amber.'

'What else did she tell you?'

'Very little, I'm afraid. Almost nothing. That's why I thought I'd come.'

'I remember the bombing. In August, the British Royal Air Force. The sirens. The bunker. The cathedral destroyed, the buildings on the island, the university where Immanuel Kant had taught. I remember the red glow in the sky. My father and brother going to see. Your mother must have been here during the bombing.'

'I imagine so.'

'How did she leave? When, do you know?'

'I don't know how she got out. She may have come later even, I'm not sure.'

W as she bombed? When did she go? Who was she? I cannot say. I know nothing.

I know a place in Cheltenham where we used to walk on the way to the fishmonger, my mother and I. For a long time there was a bombed house there that was left as it was, just one house, like a tooth lost from the street. There were places like that, in those days, places even in Cheltenham or in Gloucester where, in the war, a bomb had dropped in an air raid, and nobody had got round to rebuilding them. They were pieces of history, there before your eyes on the street. Sometimes a site had hoardings in front of it so that you could see only if you went right up and peered through the cracks. Often there was just a wire fence. Plants with lovely names grew densely in the ruins, buddleia and rosebay willowherb. In summer when the buddleias came out they collected a mass of butterflies that you would not expect to see in the centre of a town, and sometimes these flew high, wavering upwards the way a leaf floats down, to where a seed had caught in the rift in a wall and a plant somehow survived one or two floors up.

263

This particular house was gone entirely save for a single wall which stood to its full height: three floors gone but you could see where they had been, see the fireplace and the wallpaper of each room, one above the other. On the first floor the wallpaper was of a vivid green and so little damaged that you could see the pattern of it and the squares where pictures had hung. You could imagine a family sitting in the room, armchairs and a fire in the grate. I used to think about the family every time we passed, and sometimes I talked to my mother about them. Did the Greens get to the shelter before the bomb dropped? Were they still alive, all of them? Where had they gone to live? I imagined them going to save their things, if any of their things had survived, picking through the ruins afterwards in a cloud of dust.

'Yes, sweetheart,' she would say. 'I'm sure they were safe. There were warnings, and sirens, and things.' She said for sure they were in a shelter when the bomb fell.

She said it lightly, as we went on into the fishmonger's, and she talked to the fishmonger at length, and when we left she complained as she always did about the poor quality of English fish, which was never fresh as she was used to having it.

Her answer stayed in my mind because it was so light and careless and unconvincing.

264

I ask the old German where his family went, when they fled.

'We had cousins,' he tells me, 'close to Hamburg. Not in Hamburg, I am happy to say, as Hamburg also was destroyed. Our cousins were outside, but close to Hamburg. And then after that, we moved into the city. There were others there who had come like us from East Prussia.'

'What about the rest, if they had no family to go to?'

'There were programmes,' he said. 'There was a housing bureau. Arrangements were made. They were sent to camps, and people were made to give up rooms for them in their homes. Though of course there were some who did not fit in. There were people who could not settle and wandered about and did not stay. The doctors have a name for it now, the condition of people after war. There were men who used to come to the door, even years later. We would know who they were. We would give them something and they would go on their way.'

The Germans insist I visit the archive where they have been in previous years. The director is a good woman, they say, for a Russian. If there is anything to know, she will find it. When he goes out the old man walks slowly, his wife to one side taking his arm. His wife would have him take a taxi but he insists that we walk, and it is not far though it seems suddenly a world away as we step out of the rush and traffic of the Prospekt Mira into a wide avenue that is the first place I have come to in this city that is recognisably German.

'Such a shame,' he says. 'Look what they have done to it.'

And his wife looks about with bourgeois distaste and repeats, 'Look.'

He stops and holds up his stick to point.

'Imagine what sort of neighbourhood this was. The good houses, the gardens behind where there were trees and lawns and flowers. My grandfather's house was close to here. Later I will show it to you.'

Yes, I say, it must have been lovely here, and I can just about imagine it. The old German villas are grey beneath half a century of dirt. The lindens along the streets are outgrown and their roots have heaved the paving. Yet the new leaves are very green on the trees and there is a haze of buds on the lilac bushes which have seeded themselves everywhere.

This is too suburban though. This is not the kind of district where my mother lived.

'I think my mother must have lived somewhere closer to the centre. She told me about the house. She said that it went up and up, and from a window at the top you could see the sea.'

'That is not possible,' he says. 'That she could see the sea.'

'I remember her saying it. It was one of the few things she ever told me.'

'It is not possible, I tell you. We are more than thirty kilometres here from the sea.'

I am sure of the words. I want to tell this old man that he must be mistaken, however much he knows the place.

'Definitely,' he says, 'it could not have been the sea. However, she might have seen the river, and the ships there.'

'Yes of course, that must be it.'

Still I hear my mother's voice speaking of the sea.

Throughout the Cold War what had remained of the Königsberg archive lay undisturbed while the archives concerning the new city of Kaliningrad grew about it. The archivist, whose family came from Kursk in one of the first inward migrations of Russians in 1947, has been employed there all of her working life. She takes us into her office and talks for a long time, and the German translates. For the first twenty years, she says, she knew it as a place of silence and order as an archive should rightly be. The building was brand new when she first came to work in it, a tall and functional block, appropriately resembling a filing cabinet, of white-painted concrete (now turned to grey like her hair) with vertical lines of smoked-glass windows down its front and steel doors at its base. Papers went in, and registers and records were made and classified, and passed from office to office and consigned to shelves and stacks on one of thirteen near-identical floors, with little expectation, in most cases, of their ever being needed again. For in those days the principle on which the archive operated was that of the systematic disposal, rather than retrieval, of information.

There is a quality of refinement in her, a wryness, that surprises since it is in such apparent contradiction to the crude city outside.

Perestroĭka, she says, came to the archive as something of a shock. In 1992, Kaliningrad opened its borders with Lithuania. Until then the region had been entirely closed to foreigners. And suddenly people came knocking on the steel door of the archive wanting to know things. Not strange things, not secret things, but just about themselves. A first wave came then from Lithuania, Lithuanian citizens and with them German citizens who used Lithuania as a route, and a second wave of Germans came in 1995 once direct travel from Germany was permitted. Through those first years they came daily. They came with names and addresses, sometimes with the name of a father or husband or brother gone missing fifty years before. Most were old, people who had some memories of the place and of their flight or explusion, people who had reached that stage of life, she saw, when a human being wants to look back and make sense of the past. A few were the children of this generation come to find out on behalf of their parents. There were even some who came to her (and these stories she found most tragic) who as small children, in the extremity of the first Russian occupation, had been entrusted by German parents to Lithuanian families and brought up in Lithuania as Lithuanians, and came now with no more than the memory of their former German names. They came to her to ask who they had been.

It was a strange time for her. In the archive building, in the library and on the chairs in the hallway, she saw people bursting into tears. She felt then that she should have had a training as a psychiatrist, so that she could sort the contents of the human mind.

We sit in her office, facing her across her brown desk. The room has a shabby ease to it, prints of old Königsberg on the wall and plants well tended in pots, the glass-panelled door left ajar to the bigger office beyond, where women talk in Russian with a lightness that suggests that they are not speaking about their work.

'I know my mother's name, that's all.'

'She says that she does not have so very much for you.'

The archivist speaks German. The old man speaks to her in German and then turns towards me and translates into English. It gives the conversation the moves of a formal dance.

'She says that most of the books from the churches, the books of births and deaths and marriages, were taken away to Germany. These things can be found in other archives, in Germany and some in Poland.'

'So what does she have?'

The archivist's hands indicate a rectangle. A large book. Her hands and her eyes communicate directly.

'She has the postal register. I do not know what you call it precisely in English. Names and postal addresses of all the citizens of Königsberg at the time when the war began. If you know your mother's name you will surely find her family there.'

It is not a book but a box, boxes, mottled grey box files containing well-worn facsimiles, cheap photocopy pages that have been worn soft by people's fingers. Some are smudged and hard to read, dark lines and shadows of folds on them from the originals, and the type is Gothic, heavy and black.

The names are listed alphabetically, with the occupation of the head of the household afterwards, and then the address. These can be cross-referenced to another file where the listings are made by street, with floor and apartment numbers recorded, and even courtyard and alley plans. There is an admirable method and precision to these records, even though they run to 1940, into the time of the war itself.

There is no hurry. The Germans have said that they will meet me later. The archivist has brought me to this empty library with its smell of dust, and sits now at the desk at the end of the room as she is required to do. She has brought some work with her and attends to it discreetly. I do not

270

begin my search immediately but only look down the pages, beginning with the As. There is an impassive history just in the way these names are crammed together, even on the first page: *Aachener, Abe, Abel, Aberger, Abernetty, Abert, Abeszer, Abraham, Absiewicz.*

I know my mother's name as Karoline Odewald. Caroline was what everyone called her but before that she was Karoline with four syllables instead of three. Karoline Odewald was the name on the papers that she had when she married, Karoline Wyatt on the passport she brought with her to England, Caroline she became once she was there. There are six Odewalds listed. No Karoline – of course I should not have expected that since Karoline would have been only a child in 1940 – but Ernst, Fritz, Hermann, Karl, Margarete and Otto. Their occupations give no clue. I have no notion of Karoline's father's occupation, have only assumed that the family was relatively prosperous and middle class since they had a grand piano in the house. I imagine someone stereotypical, a little paunchy in a waistcoat: a professional, a lawyer, a businessman.

There is only the name to go by, and the fact of the piano, and the attic window. I have that memory my mother gave me, of the grandmother's apartment upstairs and the window in the roof with its view of ships and erroneous sea. I turn to the second file to identify the position of each street, apartment building and floor where an Odewald was recorded as living, on Radziwillstrasse, Poggenstrasse, Ungulstrasse, Balterstrasse (where two

Odewalds live side by side), and finally Margarete's address on Barenstrasse. Of the six apartment addresses, not one is above the second floor.

The archivist's grey head is bent low over the high desk as she writes, a dry rustle that has become the only activity in the room.

I have that window pinned in my mind like the pictures of childhood, like the window in the book I had with the story in it of the tin soldier, that I still have and that I used to read to my own daughter: the nursery window through which the soldier falls, from a height in a tall town house, clattering on to the cobbles of the street below. I know the high roof, the street, the ships, the sea glinting in the distance, as if they were there and I had seen them. Now I cannot distinguish memory from illustration.

There was a story my mother used to tell us about Königsberg, about the time their house was burgled. She must have told the story more than once, but there is one time in particular that I remember.

'They were not burglars,' she says, 'so much as vandals.'

'What are vandals?' asks Peter.

She is cooking our tea. Wearing an apron, neat and tidy, not a hair out of place. Her engagement ring in the bowl on the shelf where she puts it safe when she is working in the kitchen. Standing at the cooker, something on the grill, sausages perhaps or fish fingers, the sort of thing she would give us after school. The grill is at eye-level and she peers into it to see if they are done.

'People who smash things up,' she says. 'You will learn about them sometime. They were the people who smashed things up in ancient Rome. Vandals and Huns, and Huns were Germans, so maybe it was Huns. They broke in when we were away at the seaside in the summer, and we found it all when we came back, when we came with our cases and our bags and opened the door and came into the hall: everything thrown around, chairs overturned, papers from the drawers, books from the shelves. The scene of a disaster!' She takes the pan down, lays it on the cooker top.

'And do you know what was the worst thing they did? The thing that made my mother glad that my father was away, that he was not there?'

'What?'

'They had spread jam over the piano keys.'

She tells it as if it is a murder. I see a murder scene, red jam oozing across ivory.

'And she and my grandmother tried to clean it themselves, but in the end they had to call the piano makers, and the men came and took the keyboard apart on the drawing-room floor.'

Men in brown overalls now, the pieces of the piano arranged across the floor like the dinosaur bones in the Natural History Museum.

'And was it done before your father got home?'

'It was, thank goodness. He never knew.'

The archivist pauses, gives a little yawn, looks up from the desk. Does it show that I am suddenly, and for a reason that I could not explain to this woman in English any more than I could in Russian, close to tears? Does the archivist look and think: Here's another, here's another one about to weep? But the woman's look is soft, not unsympathetic.

No, I will not cry. Perhaps it was right, to give us no more of the past than that. Karoline or Caroline, it did not matter. Sea or no sea. All that mattered was that she was there, laughing, in that moment.

It is not as if I came expecting to find out anything. I came only to see the place. If I had not happened to meet the Germans, I would not even have found the archive. And what I have read means nothing. There could be any number of reasonable explanations. The Odewalds might have moved house or owned their property under another name.

I might as well go now.

And yet it is so hard to go; some compulsion, the old paranoia, edging back, all the looking for things that weren't there. The gaps. The wordlessness.

So I stay and browse the files for a while longer, just turning the pages, turning through at random. Grey pages, heavy black type. So many names. Each name a person, a family history. So many Frenzels, Hermanns, Hoffmanns. Seven columns of Hoffmanns. What if my mother's name

274

were Hoffmann; which of four hundred-odd Hoffmanns might have been my grandfather?

Or Schwarz. Schwarzes run from one page on to another. Almost a column of Schwarzes, and one at the top of the second page catches my eye. Sophia Schwarz is a name I know. *Sophia Schwarz, Witwe, Koggengasse 21.*

The discovery comes like that. It is so simple, only an idle chance. If it is a discovery.

Halfway down the previous column, a Heinrich Schwarz at the same address. *Witwe* is 'widow'; the majority of the women named as householders are listed as *Witwe*. An old woman, perhaps, Sophia Schwarz, a widow, and her son in an apartment in the same building. (One family owning two apartments. Polished brown furniture, heavy curtains and lace before the glass. Room for a grand piano.) I turn to the street listings: *Sophia Schwarz, Witwe, fifth floor; Heinrich Schwarz, SS Obersturmbannführer, fourth.*

'Excuse me, I'm so sorry, can you possibly help me?'

The archivist comes over. She does understand a few words of English, now that no one is here to translate, can even speak a few.

'Where is – where was – this street? Can you show me on the map?'

There is a big map of old Königsberg on the wall above a cabinet. The archivist points with her pen to an area just too high for her to reach.

She points to some streets in the old centre, close to the

Pregel River and the docks. (The part of the city you see in old pictures, a quarter of tall houses with long roofs and dormers in them like eyes.)

'Koggengasse. Are you sure?'

'*Ja. Hier.*'

I feel an urge to laugh. It is the shock, I suppose, and the absurdity. Absurd to have found this, that I happened to find this place, that just that page caught my eye.

'Thank you so much, that's such a help. *Danke*, I mean, *spasiba*. I will go now. *Do svidaniya*, goodbye.'

The blank steel door slams shut behind me. A building like a filing cabinet, the archivist had said. The air outside is fresh and free of the smell of dust.

I meet my friends in what they called the café down the street. Café is almost too formal a name for an enterprise that is no more than a booth, a striped umbrella and a cluster of plastic chairs on a patch of concrete at the edge of a garden long gone wild. At least there is coffee, and the afternoon is unusually mild and the spot catches the sun.

No need for me to speak at first. The old man is full of news of his own. There is an unlikely giggle in him, as if he is a schoolboy with a joke to tell. The slight hesitancy in his speech frustrates him. Now you will come and see the family house. Come and see what has become of it.

I go with them like a passenger.

We cut through the block of derelict gardens and walk a couple of streets further. The house stands on a corner. It is not at all what I had expected, but an extraordinary and elaborate suburban villa, shining and new as if it comes fresh from some architect's fantasy. A touch of baroque, a touch of *Jugendstil*. High walls about it, iron gates, security cameras and intercoms, urns, balconies, a vast silver Mercedes drawn up before a marble-columned porch.

The camera moves to watch us as we stand at the gate.

'Two years ago I came here and there were four families in the house and they used the garden for a toilet. Now look at it. You would think this was Beverly Hills!'

He laughs, too loudly. A dark-coated figure comes out of the house, glares at us where we stand.

The guard shouts something. Waves us away as if we're stray dogs.

The old man dislodges the spittle in his throat. His joke has gone sour.

'Damn these Russians!'

He is suddenly agitated. His wife takes his arm.

'My grandfather was a respected man. A judge. This was a respectable house. It is a good thing my grandfather did not live to see what happened here. He died in '43. Not the war. Cancer. It was a mercy, when you think of what came after.'

Nothing I can say but only wonder about my own grandfather, here, somewhere, who he was.

Come, the wife says. We walk on.

After a time he collects himself and asks how it went at the archive.

'It went fine,' I say. 'Thank you, it was interesting. But I didn't really find anything. I couldn't very much expect to, could I, with so little information to go on?'

What am I to tell them? That there were five Herr Odewalds, any one of whom might have been the father of Karoline. That by chance I found that there was a Heinrich Schwarz and he may have had a daughter called Sophie, who might or might not have played the piano, and a mother called Sophia who lived in the apartment upstairs. That Heinrich was in the SS. That the name is familiar to me. That I have a hunch. That there have been too many stories and I don't know my way between them.

The old people walk slowly. There is pause in such a stroll for talk, questions, confidences. But for silence also.

As long as we walk down these residential avenues the ghost of Königsberg persists about us. Karl Marx Street used to be Hermann-Göringstrasse. The tram runs just behind here, the man says. He offers the memory flatly, bitterness dissipated now. They used to get this tram to school. The line runs behind tall backs of tenements and then out on to the main thoroughfare and we are in Russia again.

In the jewellery box she kept a couple of amber neck-laces (one dark, one light, two shades of marmalade), one good string of cultured pearls, a pair of gold earrings shaped like tiny bells that tinkled when she wore them, a dozen other pairs of earrings and various costume beads of little value. Sometimes she opened the box and let me look through all its contents. The box had an inner case lined with green velvet that had separate compartments and slots into which rings and earrings fitted, and inside the lid there was another flat compartment where she kept her rosary and a few mementoes. It would have been easy to miss this compartment if you did not know that it was there, as the catch was small and concealed within the folds of the fine velvet lining.

'Where did this come from? And this? Daddy bought this for you, didn't he?'

I took things out one by one and held them up before the mirror.

My mother's laugh was dark, a depth of German in it like in her voice.

'Daddy bought them all for me, almost all. When I met him I had almost nothing but the clothes I stood up in.'

This evening she was wearing a black dress for a cocktail party. She spent ages getting dressed for a party. Sometimes I thought she went just for the excuse it gave her to dress up. She took the pearls from the box and put them on, winding them three times and fastening the delicate clasp behind her neck. The pearls were his wedding present to her, which he had given her when they first came to England.

The amber necklaces were from Berlin. I held these up now and saw how the light caught in the beads and showed up flaws. I liked the paler one best, that was like Golden Shred.

'Those come from the sea, from where we used to go for holidays.'

'But you didn't get them there.'

'No. I've told you this before, haven't I? Daddy bought them on the black market. I was with him one day and we saw this woman whom I had known before, and she was selling them. She had been a friend of my parents, rather grand, and there she was in the street in Berlin selling her jewellery. He gave her a good price, of course.'

'Because she was your friend?'

'No, not because she was my friend. Because your father is your father. He didn't even know that I knew her. But he was so soft-hearted, he always gave everyone a good price.'

'I'm going to wear these, when I'm older.'

'Have I told you about how amber is made? How old it is, how it came out of trees thousands and thousands of years ago, and how they find it now under the sea?' She had put pearl studs in her ears to go with the necklace.

'Can I keep it on when you go?'

'If you like.'

'Can I look in the secret compartment?'

'But I'm going in a minute.'

I knew what I would find. I had looked many times before. There was a tiny metal frog the size of my father's thumbnail, which came from a restaurant in Paris. They had been for a holiday to Paris once and gone to a restaurant called La Grenouille where you were given a little frog when you had paid the bill. There was a rosary which had strange brown beads like nuts and had been blessed by the Pope. And then there was the little cat that my mother had kept on all her travels, which was the only thing that came from her home and her childhood. It was a tatty thing of black fur and wire, with bendy legs and tail, and glass beads for eyes, and a ribbon round its neck with a silver medallion on it like a bracelet charm, and that name was engraved on the medallion, *Sophie Schwarz*. The letters were Gothic and hard to read.

'Why does it say that?'

'What did you say, sweetheart?' She was standing up, ready to give me a kiss and go. My father was calling from downstairs.

'Whose name is it?'

She bent and kissed me on the cheek, and then on the top of the head.

281

'Oh but it's the cat's name, of course.'

'It's a funny name for a cat.'

'What's funny about it? I think it's a fine name. *Schwarz* means black. It's a black cat.'

The jewellery box is one of the things I brought home when my father died. Even when I was a child I had always assumed that it would come to me and not to Peter. It was mine because I was the girl, my mother's daughter. The amber necklaces have gone to Peter's girls in Hong Kong. I sent them because I thought it would be a connection for them with the past, if they wanted it. I don't know if they valued the gift. Their letters of thanks were neat and formal and I couldn't tell, and Peter himself never acknowledged it. Later I thought that I should not have bothered. I should have kept them for my own daughter.

I promised Peter a postcard from Kaliningrad. There aren't many to be had here but in a little shop by the amber museum I found some of pre-war Königsberg, old images reprinted in sepia by the Russians for nostalgic Germans, who must be almost their only tourists: the lost city, the cathedral, the forts, the drawbridge over the river, even the synagogue with a group of Jewish schoolgirls posing before it. There's a street scene Peter might like, a view with the castle to one side and a road and trams and a scattering of pedestrians. It looks a pompous place, with statues of sword-bearing Prussian warriors and nineteenth-century commercial buildings.

Dear Peter, I might write, *It's not like this now. Really there's almost nothing to see here.*

That was what she said, wasn't it? When I asked her if we might go. There's nothing to see there. What should a child see? Only clean and neat and pretty things, pretty maids all in a row. No ruin, no death. Not the truth. Not things that are already buried.

Dear Peter, There's nothing to see here. The war and the Russians eradicated it all. Only guess what I found . . .

It was so smooth, her lie. *It's a black cat.* If it was a lie. She is like glass to me. Her image is smooth as glass. I could shatter it with a word. Then there will be glass, mirror pieces, shattered all about me. Splinters of her on the floor about my feet.

It is hard to sleep here. Earlier I slept a snatch, and woke up feeling shaken by a dream of glass. This room is oppressive, out of proportion; both too narrow and too tall, so that the walls seem to close in. It must have been cut out of the next room in some cheap refurbishment, the bathroom cut out of it, leaving a thin vertical space that takes the single bed and just the space to walk beside it. I have the metal window open now and the noise of the street comes in, the noise of rough cars and of a nightlife that goes on into the early morning. For a while I had the window closed. It is substantially double-glazed so that it had sealed out the sound, but that only increased the sense of claustrophobia.

I have got out of the bed and put on my coat to keep me warm. I am still aware of the faint sour smell of the room, which I notice whenever I walk into it, a smell that lasts even when you live in it, that may be the smell of use or of disuse, a hotel smell of old carpet and bodies and ancient smoke and doors that are almost always closed. A sort of smell that might hang on a person if they were to spend too long in rooms like this, alone, paying by the night. That won't wash off under the bathroom's feeble shower.

There is a small brown desk and a chair before the window. A green-shaded desk lamp that makes a pool of light. I cannot finish my postcards. I have nothing to say in them. Instead, I make notes for myself, list facts and possibilities.

There were a number of Odewalds living in Königsberg before the war, but none so far as I know living in a house like the one I remember described.

A Sophia Schwarz lived in a place that fits the description, one floor above her son Heinrich. It is possible that Heinrich had a daughter called Sophie or Sophia after her grandmother. The young Sophie (if she existed) may or may not have escaped Königsberg before or during the siege. If she did not, if she was still there when the Russians captured the city, then as the daughter of a senior SS officer she had good reason to become somebody else.

There is another point to consider which I have already noted.

Under the laws of the Allied occupation, a German citizen

could not marry a British soldier until 1947. After that a special permit was introduced, issued by the Army following satisfactory completion of a one-hundred-and-sixty-point questionnaire detailing political background. How a person's identity and background could be verified in the case of a refugee from a destroyed city under Russian occupation is unclear.

My daughter phoned today.

'I just wanted to call you. To check you're all right.'

'I'm fine. It's nice of you to call.'

'Did you find out anything?'

'I'm not sure. Maybe.'

'What?'

'Or maybe not. I don't know. I thought it mattered but perhaps it doesn't.'

'Tell me.'

'It'll take too long.'

'Tell me some of it.'

'It's a long story, I wouldn't know where to start. Don't waste your phone bill. I'll tell you when I get back.'

'Promise?'

'I just said I would, didn't I?'

'Bet you don't, when it comes to it. You'll keep it to yourself. You never tell me anything.'

'You should have come with me,' I said. All of a sudden I wished terribly that she had been here with me. 'Really you should have. I should have waited like you said, and then we could have come together, the two of us, in the summer.' A sudden fantasy: an unlikely holiday in this place, the two of us in summer clothes, sunglasses, eating ice cream in the café by the zoo.

After May 1945 in the Soviet Occupation Zone of Germany (part of which became Poland, part Kaliningrad, part the German Democratic Republic) sixteen thousand persons were charged with participation in crimes against humanity and for war crimes. These would have included many members of the SS. Many more thousands of other Germans were transported to labour camps.

The transported Germans were not returned West until 1947 earliest. An individual might only have been released sooner under the most exceptional circumstances – for example, if he or she had made some deal or was working for the Russians.

It is said that the Russians were placing spies in the West from the moment the division of Germany occurred.

There's a commotion outside. A car's brakes, a crunch of metal, angry voices. I look out to see a dark car skewed across the road, shiny beneath the street lamps, a cluster of people gathered before its lights, others crossing to the opposing pavement, walking on, heads down. Cold air. Nothing to do with me. I close the window again, draw the curtain back across it.

The chill stays with me. I see myself in this moment as I saw her, so long ago. This room is like the room I used to dream her in. In the early hours of the morning in a Soviet city, a woman stands awake in a room with her coat pulled about her. She stands at the window looking down. Sees a car below.

It was so potent, the spy story. At times I more than half believed it. It was so easy to imagine; the images, clichés all of them, so often reinforced. The adult world fed us all that spy stuff and did not know how deep it went.

Of course it didn't end there at the cemetery. I wanted to go back sometime with flowers for her. I would have picked her favourites from the garden and taken them in a jar. But that didn't stop me dreaming things.

It didn't stop Peter either. It went on building in him and in the end it drove him right away.

'Dad doesn't know anything.'

Or if he does, he has to pretend. He works for the Government, doesn't he? Maybe he's signed the Official Secrets Act. Maybe he's a spy as well, one of ours. Has to keep silent so he doesn't blow his cover.

It was just after that day Dad showed us the grave, perhaps the very next day but one of those shining summer days that one cannot connect with any preceding day of rain. Dad was in the garden, oblivious as ever. Peter was too stubborn to go out. Peter must resist even the sun. His paleness was an assertion of his determination not to accept things as they were or as others would have them.

'You don't know anything either.'

He knew that I'd be with Dad in the end. That he was the odd one out, that I was like Dad and that if he might have been close to anyone it would have been to the one person who was no longer there. (And he was right in that; Alec and I had an understanding even in our silence, from which he was excluded, and that was in our nature, in the dynamic, and there was nothing any of us could have done about it.)

'I saw her, when I ran away. I did. I saw her.'

He spoke flatly, without force. The French windows were open and there was the sound of summer outside, yet his voice resounded between us.

'You didn't. It's not true.'

He went upstairs to his room. He removed himself so completely that he didn't even have to slam the door. I heard his radio start up and knew that he had cut himself off as effectively as by any violence.

It was such a big lie he couldn't ever go back on it.

I was going to write to Peter. Give him the facts, the history and the circumstantial clues, let him make out of them what story he will. See, he could say then. Even if he does not say the words I would hear them in him and that would be the same. Peter's old dry tone. A bitter self-justification. He was right, we were right to sense that she was not who she said she was. That there was something there to be discovered. So, she might have been a spy, a plant, a sleeper, after all.

But there's more to it than that. There's something else. It comes to me now. Strange, how things can suddenly make sense in the darkness; that there can be clarity in the dark that isn't there in the day. I see how important it was. It hadn't seemed to matter much before.

'Say she's Polish, if anyone asks you, at school or any-where.'

He has come home tough from his first term away from school. He is eight, only just eight since he is young for his year. He tells me like it's great advice he's offering but I don't see the point of it.

'What's Polish?'

'If they notice her accent or anything. Polish is OK. They don't mind that. And they can't tell the difference.'

It was more than a year before she died. She was around and I might have asked her if I didn't understand, but I didn't. This was between Peter and me.

He didn't like school. He made a big fuss at the end of the holiday, before he went back. It started out by the car when everything was ready, the cases packed and the four of us standing about it ready to get in, Peter all neat in his shorts and his blazer. I didn't hear what began it. I only saw it happen, on the other side of the car, Peter suddenly with his face twisted and punching, my mother holding him, trying to hold him still; and it went back into the house, she pulled him back into the house off the road, quickly so that the neighbours didn't see, and he was kicking her and crying and trying to get away. We followed them into the hall, Dad and I, and the screaming and the row went up the stairs and along the landing and back to his room, and the door slammed and the two of them were in there, and we stood and did nothing but heard him hitting and screaming.

Nazi, Nazi!

'Stop it, Daddy. Stop him saying that.'

But he stood at the bottom of the stairs as if he was stuck there.

Then she came out and her face was red like I'd never seen it. Her hair was all messed and her print dress was torn where Peter had grabbed it.

She looked at us as though she didn't know us, or we didn't know her, ran out to the car and drove away.

Ages later, or it seemed ages later, she came back. She must have driven off somewhere and parked, and fixed her hair and her face in the driver's mirror. I could see her doing that, in a place where you could drive off the road into the woods. Head raised, taking out from her bag comb, compact, lipstick, looking herself over in the narrow strip of mirror. Doing that, and composing herself, carrying herself when she came back with such dignity that the tear in her dress hardly showed. Dad took Peter to school and I went along too. She stayed behind then and all the times afterwards, and didn't even go to the school when sports day came round.

Dad was surprisingly soft about it. I thought he would have been more angry. He got the story off Peter in the car. How when they played games at school they made Peter be a dead German. He had to be dead from the very beginning of the game, not even getting the chance to die. Just lying where they told him to be, where they said they'd shot him, on the floor or under the table or in the mud. It's not fair, he said. I don't even get to have a gun.

I have thrown away the postcard I had started. There is another that shows Immanuel Kant's death mask, which is kept on a velvet-covered pedestal in an upstairs room in the restored section of the cathedral.

Dear Peter, There's almost nothing to see here. The war and the Russians eradicated it all. All that's left are a few dismal ruins and poor old Kant, who was the only German inhabitant that Soviet ideology could permit to remain. Back to Berlin tomorrow. Love, Anna.

That's barely enough. The card's only half filled. But it will serve the purpose. I shall leave it at that. Peter has moved on, after all. Peter got away, remade himself somewhere else. He is the one who takes after her, not I.

I shall go back to bed. I shall try to sleep again now. I heard an ambulance come outside but the noise has subsided. I have set my alarm. In the morning I must wake early. I shall take a taxi, an official one that has been ordered by the hotel, back to the station, back through the last I shall see of this place. If I have not slept enough I can sleep more on the train, sleep across Poland.

5

It is the first weekend in May. I have returned to the same hotel but this morning when I came out the Berlin streets seemed quite different from before; so many people out, all dressed in fresh colours, the cafés alive on the wide pavements, upright bicycles gliding by. In the centre of the nearby platz a fat man in a red shirt was playing gentle football with a boy and it was as if they were performing for the circle of idlers on the benches and on the spring grass. There was a market around the platz; a barrel organ, bright stalls of food and clothes. I was tempted and bought a cotton blouse I saw hanging on a stall, not even trying it on. It is a bit flimsy, not really my style, but perhaps I shall wear it on a hot summer's day. It would be so light to wear in the heat, and today comes as a reminder of what summer can be.

A fresh-faced girl ran the stall. I think that she made the clothes herself.

'What a lovely day.'

'Yes,' she said. 'It has only just come like this. This is the first weekend that it has not been raining, all of this spring.

Even when there has been a fine day in the week, when the weekend comes it has not been so.'

That explains the lightness of the city. I had not expected such lightness here.

Before the Brandenburg Gate stands a man dressed and painted entirely in yellow with a yellow tulip in his hand, absolutely still. Passers-by stop and fidget and watch him, and throw money into the yellow bag at his feet.

On the other side of the Gate stands a giant sculpted car painted a solid shining silver. A girl in sunglasses climbs on to it and poses for a photograph where Russian soldiers once posed on tanks.

At the new Holocaust Memorial children play hide-and-seek within the forest of granite blocks. Their laughter travels up and down the aisles where others wander and reflect or sit and take the sun.

In the Tiergarten the lilac is out.

There was a clump of lilac in the garden at home, just where you walked through into the orchard, and my mother used to cut it, early, when the buds were fat but you could hardly see their colour. They opened fast once you brought them into the warm. There was a day like this, at this time of year but not I think such a fine day. It was just a mild, ordinary English day in May. We were in the sitting room and my mother was arranging lilac in a wide blue vase.

My mother has spread the stems on newspaper on the floor, and she cuts each one to length with secateurs and hammers the woody base as she has shown me how to do, so that it can more easily take up water. She is singing, a song without words as it seems neither German nor English.

To the memory though there are words. (If you follow a memory through, words grow in it, but you can never be quite sure whether they come from the memory or from the imagination.)

'Did I ever tell you, Anna, that we had white lilac for our wedding?'

'Did you have a white dress too?'

'No. Only a cocktail dress someone gave me, and I was up half the night altering it.'

'Then it wasn't white.'

'It was only the lilac that was white. And the snow. That was the lovely thing, you see. It was December and it was snowing. We got engaged in May but we had to wait all that time until the papers came through. Your father said that he would arrange for flowers. He was wonderfully sure about it although I could not imagine where he was going to get them from, in December. And he found lilac. It must have been grown in a hothouse. You would not have thought there could be such a thing as lilac in Berlin that time of year.'

I read this line recently: *Many trees and bushes, particularly chestnuts and lilacs, had a second flowering in Hamburg in the autumn of 1943, a few months after the great fire*. After the firestorm, the bombing, the trees flowered. The thought was deeply comforting but I could not say then precisely why.

When the girl – no, I do not see my mother as a girl, but as a young woman, by her sophistication – when the young woman comes to the city it is still winter. It is the winter of 1947 – the winter before she will be married – and the weather has been exceptionally hard. Each morning there are dead pulled out on to the pavements: the bodies of those who have frozen during the night in the cellars and shacks in which they slept. The only mercy of the cold is that it shrouds the hideousness of the ruins, of what they are, and what they represent. Snow turns rubble wastes into fields of dunes, smashed blocks into Rhineland castles. Icicles hang before gaping windows like black-market diamanté.

She wears a felt hat pulled low on her head, a scarf wrapped round her neck, a thick woollen coat belted tight. She walks tidily, briskly, picking a sure way across the patches of ice and the packed snow. She walks faster than those on the street about her, weaving past almost as if they were things; as if she does not see them, their dull eyes and their shuffling and their hunger. She passes a queue, queues. This is the morning and it is the time for queues. Almost everyone but herself is carrying something, an empty bag, a box, a bucket. She has only a small purse clenched under her arm.

She comes to an entrance, checks the address against a paper from her pocket. The building's façade has superficial damage and its number has been lost but a board has been put up to identify it. It is a substantial building. There is an archway, a hall with a staircase leading off on either side, pieces of coloured glass in the windows intact where they have been sheltered beneath the arch. Through the archway, a quiet open courtyard, and beyond that a second arch and another, smaller courtyard so narrow that the height of the building suddenly towers above the space.

Here there is a desk at the foot of the flight of stairs, a woman in uniform to check her papers and direct her to the second floor. Her papers still have a crispness to them. They will soon be so handled, in this city of checkpoints and checks and coupons and passes, that they will begin to acquire the texture of cloth.

Her steps sound on the stairs. From above comes a hum of English voices, a sound that she follows from the landing and along the corridor to the open door of the office. She is standing in the room a moment before anyone notices her. There is time to take in the strange normality of the scene, the orderly activity, the rustle of papers, the muffled thud of typewriter keys on interleaved paper and carbon, the smells of coffee and Virginia tobacco, and most of all, the warmth. It is like coming to an oasis.

The typist looks up. Hello, love, you must be the new girl they sent. Take off your coat then and tell us who you are.

Beneath the coat she is wearing a brown suit, nicely tailored. Nothing special but the typist's glance reminds her that she looks good in it. It has a prettier cut than an ATS uniform and it serves an equal purpose. Coming from what she has come from makes you appreciate the value of good tailoring. It is dignity. Identity. It is an assertion against chaos. It holds a person together.

There is tea, and sugar to put in it. Biscuits. She takes one. Here, take more than that, love, take a few. The typist puts out half a dozen on a plate. You'll be hungry. Everyone's hungry in this city, and it's all the worse, isn't it, in the cold?

She has learnt the language well. She understands what this woman says but as yet she can speak only precise monosyllables in response. It will not take her long to acquire an ease with it, idiomatic ease, though her German accent will always remain noticeable. She will be helped in this by the tall man who has a desk at the far end of the office, by the window. He will give her words, phrases, an understanding of English irony, soften her too-punctilious grammar. Yet for now he appears to be the one person in the office who has not yet seen her, sitting bent over his work with the snowlight from the window falling across him.

She speaks to him first at lunchtime, in the canteen downstairs. He is tall, but stands with a diffident hunch

301

that seems an attempt to make himself smaller. His look is vague, his smile light. He hands her a bowl of soup. He speaks to her in German that is almost perfect. He studied in Germany before the war. He is one of the few British she will meet who have a sympathy for the place, its landscape and even its people. But she does not know that yet, only she sees the hands that cup the soup bowl and the thought comes to her that if they were to touch her they would touch her softly as they would a wounded bird.

It is good that he does not ask her questions. He chats, pauses, breaks up his piece of bread and drops it into his soup. In the silences the words rise that she might but will not say. The past she has known that would answer to his past: places, sights, rooms, faces. The other past that she knows as a list, the trail of facts that lies behind a person with a particular name. He does not appear to mind what she withholds. Perhaps this is a man to whom she will never have to explain herself, with whom she can simply be. Then he speaks again. I'm not really a soldier, you know, though they've got me in uniform now. Spent most of the war behind a desk. And the first couple of years I was teaching – German, of all things – at a school in the depths of the country. He names a place that she has never heard of. She pictures it green, with hills.

She fixes on it in that moment. She will come to a place like that. In a place like that the past will be a great distance away.

* * *

302

Is that how it went? All that matters will be the present and the future, and the rest will be put away: whoever she was, whatever brought her to precisely this place, this city, this office and no other. This is what everyone is doing, all about them. What the rubble women have been doing since the moment the war came to an end, out on the streets clearing the debris, picking out from the ruins the bricks that are whole and chipping them clean, piling them in stacks ready for rebuilding, the stacks that have lined her path here this morning, that are to be found all across the city. This is what the whole world is doing: clearing, forgetting, reconstructing.

The Tiergarten lies at the heart of the city and at the centre of the devastation. The war and its aftermath have laid it bare, barer than the ravaged districts about it because of the systematic actions of men that have followed on the bombs, the axes that felled the trees, first for firing lines and later, in the winter just passed, for firewood. Their stumps stand like gravestones, receding into the flat distance. There are craters that were made not by bombs but by human hands with spades, as even the roots of the trees were dug out for burning. Areas of soil between them have been cleared, dug over to be planted with potatoes. Soon as the snow was gone the gardeners came and turned the centre of the city into a peasant field. Coated, scarved and aproned figures came and worked with bent backs, broke the ground, heaped the soil, then brought the seed potatoes they had saved even through the winter of frost and hunger, put them in around the week of Easter. There is an appropriate resurrection in the planting of potatoes at Easter.

By May their rounded leaves show above the soil. (The knowledge there to those who grow them of new tubers about to form, spread underground.) Open to the sun, the Tiergarten begins to heal. A soft green line in the distance shows where the zoo lies, where a few trees have survived though almost all of its animals are dead of starvation and eaten, many of them, by the starving. And here and there, where there are hollows and about the ponds, are remnants of thickets, and undergrowth that is all the more profuse for the loss of the canopy that used to shade it. Bracken begins to emerge, touch-me-nots, woodland plants, shining grass.

The Englishman walks beside the girl. He does not touch her and yet his step is so adjusted to hers that the connection between them is clear as if his arm is about her. His head leans to hers, just so slightly, his whole body turns by a few degrees towards her when she speaks; there is a care to him – or perhaps this is an effect produced by his height, for he is tall, much taller than she is – that suggests that he is her protector as much as her lover. The girl looks ahead, looks about her in a lively way, only sometimes looking directly to him, poised as if she is dancing in the light of the attention that he is giving her. There are other soldiers out with their girls, but this couple stand out. This particular girl is strikingly attractive, dark hair falling back in waves from her face. (She wears no hat because of the warmth of the spring sun.) And the man wears his uniform amateurishly, for he did not fight in the war, with a bookish, desk-bound look that sets him apart.

They walk past a group of Russian soldiers. In the streets and the parks here the Russians and the Americans seem to hang about in larger groups, young – many of the Russian soldiers look astonishingly young – and assertively male like teams of footballers or hunters or schoolboys. The British and the French tend to wander more thoughtfully, in pairs and threes. These Russians eye the girl quite openly, but in an appreciative rather than a predatory way. Whatever it is they say may be a compliment to her or an expression of envy at the inappropriately soft-looking Englishman who has her company. If the girl understands the Russian words, if she has spoken Russian in some other place, she does not show it. If she has suffered at Russian hands, if (like so very many) she has known the horror of Russian soldiers inside her, she does not show that either, as if her body would have been a separate thing, lined with hardness, insulated against feeling. Her senses will be open only as she wills them, to the sights, odours, tastes, touch that she chooses to know.

'So what are you thinking, Alec? Give me a penny for them, is that what you English say?' (Most of her phrases come direct from the textbooks in which she has learnt them.)

'That's what they say we say, but you don't much hear people say it. I was thinking about potatoes.'

Her laugh is clear. No one would know about the steel within her.

'No, really,' he says. And she steps before him, turns so that their bodies brush, looks up into his face.

'I was thinking that this isn't good soil for potatoes. It's too sandy here. Potatoes grow much better at Charlottenburg. Someone told me that when they laid out the Charlottenburg gardens they imported topsoil from elsewhere.'

'You weren't listening to me then, to what I was saying, before!'

'No, why, should I have been? Was it important?'

No. It was not important. She cannot even remember what it was. She sees that that is how it is with him. He likes to hear her talk but he does not listen to her words. There is a separation there that leaves her free.

They come to one of the ponds. There is lilac beside it, lilac thick beside the water.

'I have never seen,' he says, 'lilac so heavy with flower as here.' He has never known spring arrive with such raw force as in this city, this year. Or perhaps it is only because of what surrounds it; or because it is silent, because there are no birds, because the birds have gone, flown away or killed in the bombardment or eaten by the starving. 'But then this the ideal place for lilac, isn't it? It grows like a weed in this part of Europe.' She's a city girl, and hasn't noticed.

The thread of his thought is a constant beneath everything else, his observation of what interests him; his interest, here in this place, in this park in the spring, in what grows and how well it does. In years to come when they are married this will become more evident, his gardener's eye at times a joke and at times an irritation to his wife, but now his comments come to her brightly as a reinforcement of hope, as he speculates that the effect of all the destruction, the fires and the ashes, may act in the soil as a stimulant to growth.

'Close your eyes,' she says, 'and smell it. The lilac, the warm air. It makes you forget.'

When she opens her eyes, his are still closed. He looks serious like a man praying and that makes her laugh.

The pond is still and brown, bronze where the light hits the water. Where a sapling cherry has survived the bombardment and the felling, there is a light spray of petals across its surface. Black leaves show in the water at its edge. When the water is disturbed these are churned up and a smell escapes of sodden leaves and decay. There is a boy there, poking in the water with a stick. He has seen something that interests him, some piece of debris that is buried beneath last year's leaves. He is a thin boy with messy blond hair and he stands with his feet right at the edge of the pond and tries to lift whatever it is with the long stick that he has found. A man who is passing stops and watches him. That draws attention to him and some others stop also, a little further away.

'Alec, look!' She catches his arm.

Others like themselves see that something is going on, but only through the corner of an eye as they walk by, not consciously registering the event yet aware, so that if something further were to occur they would remember having seen it from the start. It is a woman who makes the move, an elderly woman who is neatly dressed in a coat and hat that are too heavy for the day. She calls to the boy with an authority that suggests that she might once have been a schoolteacher, and he looks up, holds still. She goes closer and speaks to him then, urgently, shaking her head. Slowly he lifts the stick out of the water. There are leaves clinging to it and drips falling away. He throws it down. As the water clears those who have been observing come closer. The dirt and the black leaves swirl and settle about a metal shape that could just be the casing of a shell.

The couple pull tight together now and walk away down a path that leads between two bushes of purple and paler lilac. The moment of fear has put a charge between them. In a place where the light shafts on to them, they stop and hold each other, where the grass is very green. Yet here too there are people, another couple, approaching. They seek a place where there is no one else, but in this cleared park there is no hidden place where a British intelligence officer might make love to a German girl. And so she leads him away. She leads him to where they can take a tram, out from the centre of the city to where she has her apartment, only one room and a kitchen, and nothing inside it is hers, but it is private, up shaky flights of stairs.

There is a chance on that journey that the whole thing might end, right there, when it has scarcely begun. Close to the tram stop is a market where people sell things. They come and lay things out before them on a blanket on the pavement: china, gold, watches, stockings, cigarettes in packets that are already battered with handling, a bundle of precious sticks of asparagus from the countryside. The Englishman wants to buy her a present. He stops, browses, bends to take a closer look at a piece of jewellery. All the time she does not loose the hand of his that she holds but grasps it tighter, pulling at his fingers. He, laughing, reaches back for her, puts his arm now around her waist. Here, how about this one? It is an amber necklace, a fine colour, very clear.

'How much is it?' he asks the woman there. The girl has scarcely looked at her until now. She is a middle-aged woman of tight respectability. She has brought her possessions in a suitcase, and a folding chair for herself to sit in, laid the things out on the suitcase lid. There are not very many of them but they are all good; besides the necklace, a large brooch also of amber, trinkets and scarves and pieces of lace, a clock, a cup and saucer that may perhaps be Meissen. She has been sitting with that hunched anonymity that so many of the market traders have, that is part boredom, part a removal of herself from the fact of what she is doing there. It is only now, with the possibility of a sale, that she becomes alert, and the girl looks into her face and knows her from the past.

She is certain that the woman must recognise her also. This woman has known her all of her life, but as another person under another name. Yet she does not say it. She looks away, looks now only at the Englishman and names a price, and it is the high sort of price you would name to a British soldier who appears to be in love. Then when he does not bargain she unclasps her bag and takes from it a scrap of tissue paper that she has smoothed and folded from its previous use, and wraps the necklace in it, and takes the notes he gives her and folds them and puts them away. And lets the girl go on being the other person that she has become, and the girl goes on and does not know whether the woman has acted out of discretion or amnesia.

The boy with the stick stands idle, looking out across the pond. A roller skater comes up behind him, then another, two youths who are bigger, bulkier, than he is. The second brushes so close behind him that he takes a step forward, almost to the water's edge. He shouts something angry after them, throwing down his stick. Then scuffs away, hands in his pockets. He goes right past me where I sit on this bench in the sun.

A NOTE ON THE AUTHOR

Georgina Harding is the author of the novel *The Solitude of Thomas Cave* and two works of non-fiction: *Tranquebar: A Season in South India* and *In Another Europe*. She lives in London and the Stour Valley.

A NOTE ON THE TYPE

The text of this book is set in Granjon. This old-style face is named after the Frenchman Robert Granjon, a sixteenth-century letter cutter whose italic types have often been used with the romans of Claude Garamond. The origins of this face, like those of Garamond, lie in the late fifteenth century types used by Aldus Manutius in Italy.